I0599086

UNICORN SHIFTER ACADEMY

BOOK 1

USA Today Bestselling Author

J.R. THORN

Unicorn Shifter Academy: Book 1 © 2022 by J.R. Thorn

Cover Art by Rebecca Frank
Title Page by Elena Sova
Chapter Header Art by Ricky Gunawan
Illustration by Ricky Gunawan
Edited by Love2Read Romance

ISBN: 978-1-953393-10-4

To my readers, I researched horse anatomy so you didn't have to.
You're welcome.
I'm scarred for life, but at least the Unicorn Shifters are anatomically accurate...

TASTE THE RAINBOW HAS A WHOLE NEW MEANING...

There are three rules at Unicorn Shifter Academy.

1. Keep unicorns a secret.
2. Never compare horn sizes.
3. No girls allowed.

Whoopsie. I broke all three.

You'd think that unicorn shifters would be chicks, right? Yeah, me too, but turns out unicorns are always males.

Until me, that is.

I've never shown a drop of magic in my life, even though I'm from a family of powerful witches. Well, my parents had the grand idea of performing an awakening ceremony courtesy of Fortune Academy's best and brightest… and I think it worked a bit too well. Imagine their surprise when I sprouted a horn. A FREAKING HORN.

Not. Cool.

Turns out there was some serious rainbow hankypanky in my family history and now the unicorn shifters are pissed off I'm in on their secret community.

Seriously, spilling the magic beans is the least of my worries.

Being a unicorn means bonding with seven other shifters for life—a life I never asked for. And since I'm the first girl in a male-only tradition, I expect this could cause some serious problems, especially because these guys are obsessed with me right off the bat. Like overly protective to the extreme. A girl can take care of herself, you know?

Thing is, we better get our act together because this Academy isn't just for show. Unicorns are the only creatures who stand between good and evil on a

cosmic scale. A monster lurks in a terrifying pit in
the center of the Enchanted Forest.
And it looks like somebody let it out.

The clock starts now to trap the beast before it eats
my home realm as a snack. I've got my big girl
panties on—even if they are rainbow-colored.

AUTHOR'S NOTE

Welcome to *Unicorn Shifter Academy: Book 1!*

This is a standalone series written in the Blood Stone Universe.

If you're new to my books, you'll be happy to learn that I write all my series in the same world and they can be read in any order. You'll see familiar characters over and over again, so you'll never have to truly say goodbye!

If you would like to read the books in order, follow this quick cheat sheet listed on the Amazon's Sales page for any book in this universe:

Series	Series 1	Series 2	Series 3	Series 4	Series 5	Series 6
	Seven Sins	The Vampire Curse	Fortune Academy	Dark Arts Academy	Moon Guardian: Crescent Five	Unicorn Shifter Academy

Open your bag of Skittles and get your horns ready...

Welcome to Unicorn Shifter Academy.

BONNY

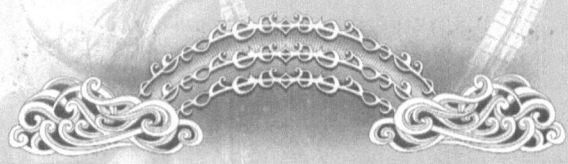

"GREAT, SKITTLES AGAIN," I grumbled as I stared at the colorful flattened orbs melting on my palm.

Why was it hot as balls in here, anyway?

"Eat them and behave," my mother chided, pushing my hand at me and glaring until I gobbled up the sugary treats.

This had to be the most bizarre day of my life.

Minus the two other awakening ceremonies my mother had dragged me to, of course.

Those were just as fucking weird, and they'd likely be just as fruitless.

Crunch.

The irony was not lost on me that these Skittles were fruit-flavored.

As if that can cover up the magical sour taste these leave in my mouth. A for effort.

Taking my time, I chewed up the sugary goodness and tried to pretend they were just regular treats, minus the tangy aftertaste.

The lingering sensation assured me that they weren't just any regular candies. That became abundantly apparent when my extremities began to tingle. And not the good kind of tingles like when I drank soda too quickly and my eyes burned.

What a great way to ruin one of my favorite candies, I lamented. Needles spread throughout my body and the sweats began. Before my mother could see the offensive droplets, I wiped the back of my hand across my forehead.

I hated this.

Not to mention trying to unlock powers that weren't there was a massive waste of time. Although, I'd long ago come to that conclusion before we'd walked onto Fortune Academy's Earth Campus.

Magic hummed in the air, which reminded me of bees and only added to the sensation of a thousand stings radiating throughout my body, and my head immediately began to throb.

They know what they're doing, my mother had told me.

I glanced around, taking note of the dwarf, the tall, scantily dressed female Dark Mage with black eyes, and what had to be a vampire sloshing a red glass of wine that was way too thick to be actual wine.

Great, I thought with a frown. *I hope I don't turn out to be a vampire.*

This was the most esteemed supernatural Academy in the world, and since the realms started merging, it attracted all sorts of interrealm species.

Everyone wanted to learn from the best. Boys practically creamed their pants at the thought of catching a glimpse of one of the Champions of Calamity.

I hated to be the one to tell them that the days of the Champions were over. According to the latest news, a new era of peace had begun.

At least, that was the propaganda regarding peace. I didn't believe it for a second.

Nothing about being force-fed poisoned skittles felt *peaceful.*

When I looked across the auditorium, I saw scared teenagers and entitled, supernatural parents trying to keep their little self-fabricated thrones.

Magic was the new currency in our world, and whoever had the biggest, most powerful family with the most outrageous type of gifts made them the top dogs.

Or top witches, as it were.

My mother was basically a Queen, and that was the only reason I was standing here right now even though I didn't have a magical bone in my body.

I couldn't have felt more out of place.

The walls shimmered with magically projected portraits of all of the powerful women who had failed to stop Calamity's effects, but had a fuck-load more magic than I ever would.

Renee, the Keymaster of Heaven, Hell, and Earth.

Sonya, the Queen of Hell.

Evelyn, the Ruler of the Royal Covens.

Lilith, Sonya's daughter and one of the most powerful Champions, the woman who stopped Lucifer from ruling Earth.

And then there was Ayla. They didn't share her portrait, but rather a crest of a rose surrounded by thorns fluttered against the wall. Maybe she was the shy type. Either way, I could practically taste the magic wafting from the staff that was still handing out candies, whispering spells over them before giving them to the attendees.

Fortune Academy had campuses all over after dealing with Lucifer and Calamity. Earth's campus was a prestigious place for the supernaturals left-over in the wake of the Rise.

That's what they called it; the near-extinction of everyday mortals was looked at as a blessing instead of the curse it was.

I liked being human, personally.

But in the L'estelle family, being human was an insult.

All of the nineteen-year-olds in the stuffy auditorium had the same problem and the same melted treats.

They were mortal.

Dull.

Unmagical—practically a crime these days.

The spelled Skittles that wandered down my digestive tract instantly made my stomach roll in retaliation.

My cheeks bulged when nausea wound through my stomach. I wanted to rid my stomach of the foreign contents that made me clench my fingers into my abdomen. Not to mention my head was starting to kill me.

"Don't you *dare* throw that up!" my mother hissed, sharply grabbing my arm as if she could put the fear of the gods into me enough to make this somehow work.

"I'm not," I grumbled before I took a deep breath. It didn't help.

"Good," she snapped, yanking me again for good measure. "Your father had to sell our west coast house for those."

I resisted rolling my eyes, but I rolled them internally.

Hard.

Oh no, not the beach house, I mused to myself.

The L'Estselle family had done pretty well for themselves once supernaturals were out of the proverbial bag. We'd already been wealthy, but once my family stopped having to hide that they were all a group of powerful witches and warlocks, the money *flowed.*

Something that my mother took pride in, given what she was. She straightened and swept back her hair that always floated around her face as if she conjured an invisible breeze on a constant basis.

She was an elemental, a rare type of witch who controlled nature and she made bank selling her rain to farms.

And if anyone pissed her off? They could expect to encounter a dry spell for the indefinite future.

Like an advertisement, rain droplets beaded around her flawless collarbone, creating a unique necklace, while her bleach-blonde hair floated over her shoulders.

Her pristine silver-white eyes slanted my way when I hiccupped, her delicate frown chiding me for even thinking of rejecting the magical candy.

It was supposed to activate dormant supernatural cells in my body, and after the Rise, everyone was supposed to have them.

Except this was the third time we'd tried an Awakening Ceremony, and even though my mother had spared no expense to get me into Fortune Academy this time, I had a feeling it still wasn't going to work.

Because there was nothing special about me.

I'd been trying to tell her that for years.

"Why is it so fucking hot in here?" I complained as sweat ran down the back of my neck. I gathered my hair at my nape and twisted it into a ball, taking a pencil and stabbing it through the strands to keep them in place.

"Language," my mother chided as she went to one of the cocktail tables and snatched up a new pencil that she then shoved into my hand. "They're going to start the ceremony soon. Focus."

Twirling it over my fingers—desperately wishing it was a switchblade instead of a pencil so I could stab my eyes out—I followed my mother to the row of chairs that faced the stage.

A large pedestal with a magical book rested at the center. The tall, skinny woman took the stage and smiled at us as she smoothed out the pages.

"Hello, everyone. I'm Professor Olivia." She smiled, her sweet demeanor at odds with her soulless black eyes. Her white hair was peculiar, but she had to be some sort of Dark Mage. She nodded to the dwarf who'd joined her at her side. "This is Professor Payne. He was involved in my awakening when I was a Fortune Academy student, so I can promise you all that you're in good hands with us today."

I glanced up at my mother, but she wasn't looking at me. Instead, she stood regal and proud, her little upturned nose in the air as she stared down it at the stage.

Somehow, she made herself look like she was in charge even though she was just my over-eager mother.

None of my friends were here, not that I had many. I missed Ned and Angel, two friends I'd had since diapers.

They were brother and sister and had already gone through their awakening ceremonies. It only pissed my mother off more that I was the odd one out in our little social group of elites.

A magical clipboard floated around the room. Each of us signed our voluntary participation—although mine was under extreme protest.

That done, Professor Olivia began calling names in alphabetical order. I wasn't sure if I was going to be called up with the "L's" or the "E's" given my last name was L'Estselle.

I hoped the Ls.

It would give me enough time to calm my rolling stomach—because right now it was making a gods-awful sound like a tiny animal was dying inside my gut.

Rrwaaarrrrrrr.

My mother shot down a glare. "Stop that," she hissed.

I bit the inside of my cheek to keep from replying.

Maybe if she hadn't force-fed me poisoned Skittles and ruined my favorite candy while trying to kill me, my digestive tract wouldn't be inventing new sounds.

To my disappointment, I was called up with the E's right when my vision started to spin.

Great.

Feeling like I was going to puke all over the professors, I hurried up to the stage and leaned on the podium, my fingers grazing the book as I tried to support myself.

The lights blaring overhead weren't helping the headache that was quickly approaching the worst migraine of my life.

Professor Olivia gave me a concerned glance, then placed her hand over mine. "Just hang in there, sweetie. The awakening process is easier than it used to be, but it can still be rough."

I huffed a laugh. "Unless it used to be dying, I don't think it could be much worse than this."

She blinked at me a few times, then gave me a knowing smile as if I'd said something funny.

I don't get these people.

Unfortunately, I hadn't been paying attention, so I hadn't seen how the awakening had gone for the other students ahead of me.

So far, on the other side of the stage, I spotted a wolf, a male with horns and a tail, and a girl with a victorious expression and cat-like eyes.

It seemed like it was shifter night. That didn't bode well for me.

Animals had a strange sort of obsession with me.

Like, seriously. I had to keep my windows closed or birds would come in. Little bunnies like to build nests in my pillows, and anything furry could be found attempting to break into my backpack when I'd been in high school.

Graduation had been amusing when a pair of pigeons had attempted to nest in my hair.

It was a problem, and it was exactly why my mother thought I surely had some sort of shifter or witch abilities in my blood.

I knew the truth, though. Humans were a dying breed and animals sensed my normalcy and sought me out.

I was special because I was actually *not* special.

"Put your hand here," Professor Payne, the dwarf growled at me and I glanced down to find the bearded male barely up to my chest. He held a flat stone aloft and stared at me until I complied.

Professor Olivia gave me another comforting smile, which might have actually been comforting had her eyes not been completely black.

It made her look rather terrifying.

"Try not to move, sweetie," she said and, to my

relief, closed her eyes as she began the awakening spell.

"Oh, fuck," I groaned as I doubled over. My stomach rolled and retaliated, but I kept my hand on the stone the dwarf presented to me.

"Don't remove your hand," he snapped. "This is a stone from the awakening arena and has been doused with the blood of a thousand deaths. They died so you didn't have to!"

Apparently hearing I was touching a sacrificial stone with a thousand deaths' worth of blood was not what I needed to hear right then.

My stomach heaved and my worst nightmare came true.

I puked.

Well, sort of.

I released a massive burb, except it came out in the form of rainbow bubbles.

The release seemed to help my headache, at least.

It came up until the bubbles were everywhere and the auditorium broke down in laughter.

"She's a fairy!" one voice suggested.

"No, she's a dud!" another voice shouted.

I agreed with the latter, although at the moment I was too busy expelling bubbles onto the stage.

"Bonny Magic L'Estselle!" my mother shouted,

storming onto the stage and gripping me by the arm until I was certain she'd leave a hand-shaped bruise. And, yes, my middle name was magic. Wishful thinking on my mother's part. "What in the gods' names do you think you're doing?"

Puking my rainbow guts out? I thought, but I could only hiccup one more massive bubble that popped all over her face, leaving rainbow glitter shimmering over her cheeks.

She blinked at me a few times, then drew out a handkerchief from her purse to wipe herself off.

"Do you have any idea what's going on with my daughter?" my mother asked the dwarf. She looked at the Dark Mage when he didn't answer, but she was still chanting and had both hands placed on the book.

Which seemed to be the source of the bubbles coming out of my stomach.

"Stop—*hic!*—chanting!" I begged her.

She stopped mid-chant, then opened her eyes for the first time and her dark orbs went wide in surprise.

"Well, that's new," she said.

No shit.

The dwarf peeled my hand off of the stone and narrowed his eyes at me as if waiting for something.

One more hiccup, and this time the bubbles finally stopped.

Silence engulfed us and I desperately wanted to be anywhere else in the world, anywhere else in all the realms, right about now.

Finally, Professor Olivia patted me on the shoulder. "I'm afraid it didn't work, dear. You're simply—"

My mother finished her sentence. *"Human."*

BONNY

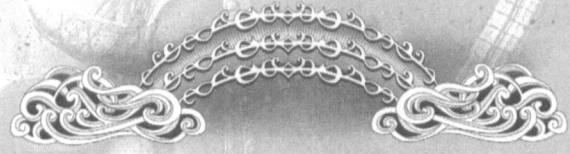

"You did not!" Angel whisper-shouted as I buried myself under blankets in my bedroom.

I was going to hide from the world for as long as physically possible.

Chatter from downstairs mulled on, informing me that I wouldn't be allowed to stay out of sight for long. My mother had organized a party in my honor. She'd been so confident that this would be my big awakening, and now what were we going to say to all of our guests?

I was nothing more than a glorified bubble-burp machine?

"It was horrible," I grumbled as I shoved another pillow over my face, attempting to smother myself out of existence.

Even though my migraine had come back with a vengeance, this time it seemed intent on driving a nail straight through my skull.

The nausea was competing for top bid in the misery department, though.

I wasn't sure who was winning.

It certainly wasn't me.

There were probably still bubbles floating around in my stomach. My abdomen gurgled and growled every few seconds, letting me know exactly how it felt about the poisoned Skittles I'd eaten.

Angel ripped the pillow and blankets off of me, her features wound up in a delighted smile. I squinted at my bedroom lights I'd insisted we keep at half-power. Luckily my family believed in dimmer switches.

"I would have paid good magic to have seen that," she said, playfully slapping my leg. "I can't *believe* you didn't invite me!"

Rolling my eyes, I sat up against the headboard and began plucking at the threads of a decorative pillow. "It was at Fortune Academy. You couldn't have gotten in anyway, even if I *had* invited you."

She drew in a long gasp. "*The* Fortune Academy? And you burped up bubbles? Holy shit. What did your mom say?"

Angel excitedly blinked at me while I contemplated the look of disappointment I recalled on my mother's face.

Angel was everything I wasn't.

She was beautiful, especially now that she'd been awakened as a mermaid shifter. She was a water sign, so that really didn't surprise me.

I'd never heard of mermaid shifters in particular, but there were a lot of new supernaturals popping up after the Rise. They were apparently different than reborn mermaids that never walked on land, and had been a myth to the supernatural community until a few recent sightings.

Angel's impossibly blue eyes glittered as if the ocean roared in her twinkling irises. Tiny scales adorned her cheeks like pink blush, and small gills ran up the sides of her neck, flaring every few moments.

Her hair always appeared a little wet and shimmery since her awakening, but it was a good look on her.

And plus the silky strands had turned bright purple. I was super jealous. I had to die mine pink.

"My mom called me *human*," I said, frowning. I was supposed to be proud of that, but being around Angel right now made me feel like shit.

I went back to plucking the strands on my pillow and closed one eye to help stem the migraine.

I don't want super special powers, anyway.

Angel placed her hand on my arm and her touch instantly calmed me.

"No mermaid magic," I complained at her, although it felt better than the needles still zinging over my skin.

She left her hand right where she'd put it and adorned a little pout on her face. "I don't like seeing you sad, though."

"I'm not sad," I insisted as I peeled off her hand.

"Didn't you want to be human?" she asked, tilting her head.

"Yeah, of course." Humans were all but extinct these days. In a weird way, that made me special.

Although, I wasn't feeling very special at the moment.

I went back to plucking the strands of the pillow when my stomach rolled. "I just don't feel so good. They gave me poisoned Skittles and they're still bothering me.

Angel hummed in thought, but she didn't get a chance to reply. The door slammed open and we both turned, startled, to find Ned grinning at us like an idiot.

Being Angel's brother, I would have loved to make fun of him for being a male mermaid, except he'd awakened as a warlock.

And he loved to show off.

"The fun has arriiiiived," he sang as he snapped his fingers, summoning his grimoire and a burst of confetti.

Typically, grimoires were only assigned to Dark Mages, but Ned wasn't like most warlocks. He wasn't like most *people*.

This was apparent because his "grimoire" was extremely unique. It was essentially a black book where he'd spelled all the original pages to turn into incantations, and the outside had his homemade clan icon, which was just a circle with a line through it.

Because the clan didn't exist. He was the first—and only—of his kind.

He called himself a rockstar warlock. Just because he played electric guitar—rather poorly, I might add—and he'd awakened as a warlock, did not give him the right to invent such a ridiculous clan.

"Not now, Ned," Angel chided.

I glared at the glitter on the floor which I realized was in the shape of tiny dicks.

"Mature, Ned," I grumbled, although a flicker of a smile edged at my mouth.

My friends knew how to cheer me up.

"Soooo, does that mean you want me to stay or go?" he asked, jabbing one thumb over his shoulder while he tucked his grimoire against his chest.

"Bonny, are you up there? We're about to make the toast!" a female voice shouted up the stairs, one of the servants who'd been my nanny for years that I called Auntie Linda.

I sighed at Ned. "Can you turn a room full of supernatural dicks into confetti instead of turning confetti into dicks?"

He chuckled as he slipped inside and closed the door. "Afraid not. Even if everyone downstairs is a certified dick, I can't turn them into confetti. My clan has a no-harm-no-foul rule."

Angel smacked his shoulder when he sat on the bed and squirmed between us. "You don't even have a clan, you dork. Stop making up rules to excuse your lack of real magical ability, unlike some of us who actually *are* rare and magical creatures." She blinked her third eyelid as a demonstration.

"Don't blink that slimy eyelid at me!" he shouted, crisscrossing two fingers in an "X" gesture.

I hiccupped, released a massive rainbow bubble

into the air, and then promptly grabbed my throbbing head.

Last time releasing rainbow bubbles had helped my headache, now it only seemed to make matters worse.

My friends both stopped and stared at the sphere while it floated across the room before bursting over the confetti dicks.

"What the fuck was that?" Ned asked, looking at me as if I'd grown two heads.

Which probably would have been less weird than hiccuping up bubbles.

"I thought I was done with this shit," I said with a groan as I rubbed my forehead. The pain seemed strangely isolated between my eyes and up a few inches. "It feels like someone has a dagger right *here*," I said, pointing to a specific spot.

A shrill voice called my name again, but it was my mother this time.

"You can't go down there like this," Angel said.

I couldn't agree with her more. That is until she jabbed Ned and clarified she was referring to my lacking attire. "Spell her into something more suitable."

"Angel!" I hissed. "I'm not going down there."

She frowned. "Look, I know this sucks, but

there's got to be a doctor down there somewhere who can help you with this. It's better than sitting up here being miserable." She raised an eyebrow at my polka-dot pajamas. "I think we'll have better luck finding help if you don't look like you just rolled out of bed, while we're at it."

The moment I'd come home, I promptly ripped off the clothes my mother had picked out for the awakening ceremony and donned my fluffiest pajamas. It wasn't my fault I preferred comfort.

"She doesn't look like that!" Ned said. When I was about to thank him for defending me, he held up my bunny slippers and whispered a spell that had them bouncing across the floor and onto my feet. "There, *now* she looks like she just rolled out of bed."

Angel gave Ned her best evil eye, which would work on anyone. Especially when her pupils turned into slits.

He visibly shivered. "Fine, fine. Don't do the eye thing. I'll spell her an outfit."

Ned shooed me into place and I reluctantly stood in front of the mirror.

My pink hair frizzed out in all directions, mostly where I'd been grabbing at it thanks to my lovely headache. My polka-dot pajamas ballooned out from my body, the fluffy cotton my preference over whatever Ned was going to summon for me.

Wiggling my toes inside my warm bunny slippers, I frowned when they transformed into knee-high biker boots.

What the...

Angel shouted at Ned while he howled with laughter, my outfit promptly transforming into a goth chick ensemble.

A short skirt with chains for a belt adorned my waist.

A tight-fitting blouse hugged my curves.

Black, sheer sleeves with holes in them covered my arms.

And even a strange silver tattoo appeared in the place on my forehead that felt like it was on fire.

The last part didn't seem to match the theme, but Ned wasn't the best warlock and magic sometimes had a mind of its own.

"Change her outfit, Ned," Angel insisted while he tried to compose himself. He rolled on the floor and wiped the tears from his eyes.

"But you should see the look on your face! She's perfect! I have my first groupie!"

Aiming for his balls, I went to kick him with my massive biker boots. "In your dreams!"

He summoned a giant stuffed bunny to catch my kick before I could do any damage—like I knew he would. Well, I didn't know he'd summon a stuffed bunny, but Ned always managed to avoid trouble. It was a game we played that kept us on our toes.

The door swung open in that instant, Auntie Linda taking in the scene before she pinched the bridge of her nose. "Your mother isn't going to like this. Do you realize who's downstairs?"

Ned struggled to his feet while Angel yanked on his arm, trying to get him upright. Meanwhile, I winced at Auntie Linda's tone. She wasn't much older than my mother, and she'd practically raised me. Elegant black hair was drawn back from her face, forming the tidy bun she preferred in the back. The only new adornment was glittering crystals she's woven into her hair. I caught a glimpse of them when she turned her head to glower at Ned.

"Are you responsible for this, Ned? I know Bonny doesn't have an outfit like that in her closet." She was responsible for maintaining my "allowed" outfits. We often argued over skirt length and if the colors I preferred were "too vibrant."

Which was why I dyed my hair pink in retaliation.

My childhood friend winced and rubbed the

back of his neck. "We were just messing around and—"

My nerves got the best of me as I released a massive burp and a rainbow bubble floated toward the ceiling. I jabbed it with a finger, popping it before Auntie Linda could spot it.

She raised an eyebrow at me. "I hope you can mind your manners when you're downstairs."

"Never mind that," I said. "I saw the invite list," I continued, hoping I could distract her from the rainbow glitter shimmering in the air. "It's just some of the lower members of the Royal Coven families and alt-realm extended tribes." Ever since the realms had merged there were more witches than the Royal Covens could handle. It was a source of contention where the jurisdiction rested since some families were forced to live in this realm now where they didn't belong.

Like my mother.

She was an Elemental from another world, not that she ever talked about it much. She'd built a life here and loved my father—that was her only redeeming quality. She missed him, and without him to bring out the good in her, she threw herself into political power struggles with an aggressive determination that often frightened me.

Regardless, I stayed out of supernatural politics as much as possible, but I knew the names I'd seen on the list weren't anyone who'd care much about me. They all wanted to kiss my mother's ass and win her favor.

Which was exactly why there had been a party in my so-called honor. My mom just wanted any excuse to rub noses and talk about how great she was. She'd probably somehow find some way to spin my human status to her favor. She did love playing the victim.

"There's an addition that *wasn't* on the list," Auntie Linda said. The sharp tone in her voice suggested it was someone important—maybe even dangerous. "He's a UMC species and says he's here to see you."

Angel bounced on her feet. "An Unidentified Magical Creature? How exciting!" She grabbed my hands. "Come on! Let's go meet him! I bet he's something cool." Her third eyelid flashed as her excitement got the best of her.

I bit my lip and looked down at my outfit. "I can't go like this."

Ned plopped his book on the bed and flipped the pages. "I'm on it!" He grumbled a bit before finding whatever he was looking for, then he placed one hand on the top of my head while he chanted.

I glowered at him. "Just because I'm short doesn't mean you can cast spells through my head—"

"Shh!" he said, then went back to chanting.

A tingling ran over my body, concentrating briefly on the place on my forehead that still burned and tickled. A sharp pressure radiated there, making my headache worse.

"It hurts," I complained, and I knew it wasn't supposed to. Something was wrong.

Does this have anything to do with those poisoned Skittles? Maybe I should go to a doctor...

A flash exploded in the next instant, my outfit transforming into something I didn't think Ned had picked.

An adorable skirt with rainbow trim, and an extremely inappropriate top that showed my entire midriff. A black top that hugged a pink under bra. Black leggings ran down my thighs, with rainbow accented side stripes, and pink underwear peeked out the top.

"Cute," Angel said, then winced. "Although, not exactly appropriate for introductions."

"It doesn't matter," Auntie Linda said with a sigh and tugged my arm. "Just get downstairs!"

She yanked and I was forced to follow her. "Slow down!" I screeched as I tumbled down with her. I didn't think falling flat on my face and breaking my nose would be a good first impression with a UMC. We hadn't had any new supernaturals appear in years, so the fact that I was keeping the bubbles in my stomach from coming out again was an achievement.

The hum from downstairs fell into silence as Auntie Linda shoved me forward.

I spotted him immediately. A male with ruby red eyes that seemed to see straight through my soul.

Not a vampire, I immediately decided. While a vampire also typically had red eyes, it was the kind of red that glowed with stolen lifeforce.

This creature's eyes glowed with an aura of raw magic and a goodness I couldn't explain.

Hope.

Ferocity.

Allure.

The sensations conveyed by his gaze hit me all at once as I took in the rest of him. His billowing cape did little to hide his muscular and powerful frame.

A hood wrapped over his head, but I spotted something else strange about him. A silver mark crested his forehead, almost like a scar.

But what frightened me was that it matched the mark that had appeared on my *own* forehead.

Pain lashed through my skull and collected at my temples, making me grab my head as I cried out in pain.

"What's the meaning of this?!" my mother shouted. She rushed through the crowd as she pushed aside Royal Coven's witches. They wore their best finery to this occasion, but I knew it wasn't for me. My mother was a powerful and rare Elemental and she was the one that everyone was supposed to be interested in.

I wasn't special.

I was human.

I was dull, uninteresting.

... *Right?*

Just when I thought my mother was concerned about my well-being, she started tugging at my shirt and plucking at the strap of my top. "What *are* you wearing?"

Of course. She wasn't concerned that my skull was about to split into two.

My outfit was the entirety of her focus right now.

She lifted her lip and plucked at my bra strap.

Her reaction felt unwarranted. It wasn't like I'd decided to waltz downstairs naked.

Which probably would have been a better idea, because right now I felt like I was the center of this male's attention and part of it had to do with my outfit.

His ruby eyes raked over my frame, taking in every inch of me and making the turmoil in my stomach ramp up a notch.

Being the sole focus of his scrutiny made me feel like a butterfly trapped in a net.

My vision blurred and rainbows exploded everywhere. Pain sliced through my skull and I whimpered.

It was something about his presence that pushed me and threatened to destroy my world.

That's when everything began to go dark and my vision blanked.

The male rushed for me as I faltered. He held me upright before yanking me against his chest.

He didn't say a word.

But it was too late, I felt our similarities just as a massive spike of pain stabbed through my forehead.

A new weight made my head tilt down and the room erupted in a massive, collective gasp.

I blinked a few times as my vision cleared, then

reached up to touch something that definitely didn't belong there.

I spotted my reflection in the two-story mirrors my mother had installed in the ballroom— because it allowed the guests to watch themselves. They all loved looking at their own images.

My image, however, didn't make any fucking sense.

Because a golden horn protruded from my forehead.

"I'm... a fucking unicorn? Are you kidding me?"

RAZE

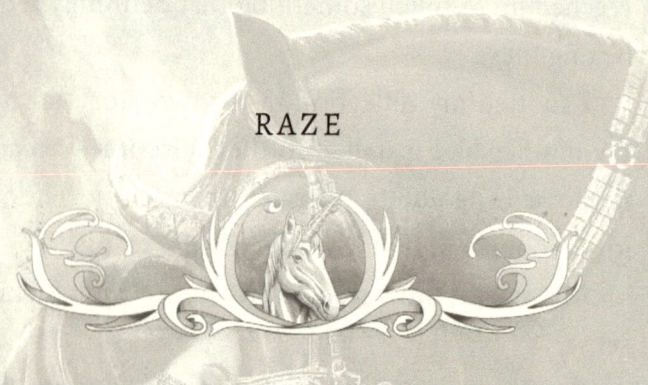

THIS WAS ABSOLUTELY UNPRECEDENTED.

I stared at the gorgeous female who had sprouted the largest, most elegant golden horn I'd ever seen in my life.

Her body pressed against mine as she still wavered from the impact of awakening her inner power.

And as a unicorn, her power was unprecedented. I needed to return her to the only realm that could contain our brand of magic before it consumed her.

She groaned, the sound going straight to my dick.

Then she leaned into me, clearly dizzy, but her breasts brushed my chest and her breath kissed my neck. Goosebumps immediately sprouted over my arms.

Fuck.

"Don't move," I warned her as I gripped her shoulders. It forced her to stay close to me, but also assured me that she couldn't do that horrible and wonderful thing again.

An unfamiliar but *unmistakable* tingling of lust stirred in my gut, startling me.

Because I wasn't supposed to feel sexual energy.

Unicorns weren't permitted to feel desire of any sort, until we gave up our magic, of course. That was because our magic ran on purity and selflessness. Like all unmated Unicorn Shifters, I'd given my soul to the Unicorn's treasure hoard to amplify our power and to protect my own gifts. It gave me the benefit of not having to deal with sexual energy or distractions, which made my feelings now all the more disturbing.

But I liked it...

And that frightened me most of all.

The female's mother stared at her daughter. I knew it was her mother because they shared the same gorgeous blue eyes that reminded me of a sunny day in my home realm. Whenever I gazed up through the trees in the Enchanted Forest, the brilliant blue of my realm's skies was like a crystal and couldn't be compared to anything else.

Until now.

This female had become my sky, had become my center, and the desire to protect her exploded within me—along with other disturbing sensations.

It didn't make any sense, but I'd learned to listen to my instincts through my thousand years.

I'd been waiting for something during my long life.

Perhaps it wasn't *something*, but *someone*.

"You're going to have to come with me," I told the female. That was obvious, but I felt the need to say something out loud. The silence crushed in on us, making me uncomfortable, and I wasn't used to the spotlight.

I wasn't even supposed to be here, much less reveal my species. However, I'd detected Purity magic being used outside our realm, and no other Unicorn Shifters were on the roster to be on Earth.

Which meant there was a new Unicorn being born.

I had expected a baby, not a fully grown female.

Much less one who made me *need*.

"Excuse me, whoever you are, but my daughter isn't going anywhere," her mother snapped. She jolted into an authoritative posture that made me immediately dislike her.

She thought she was in charge here.

"Um, hello?" the exquisite female weakly complained as she leaned into me again. She pointed at the golden horn that had graced her head.

It was remarkable, really. She'd managed a partial shift, something that took concentration and practice. Yet, she'd burst with Purity magic when she'd come too close to me, her need to shift likely overwhelming her senses.

Fascinating.

I realized that the female had been talking, so I attempted to pay attention.

She rubbed her temple, clearly agitated by something her mother had said. "Can we focus on what's important here? Like what the fuck just happened to me?"

She's got a mouth on her. I like it.

A low chuckle escaped my throat, earning a glare from the gorgeous female. I tried to cover it by pushing her away from me. Although I only managed to put her at arm's length. The desire to take her into my arms again wasn't logical. She'd stabilized from her first surge of Awakening, but more power surges would come.

Still, I didn't want to overwhelm her. Right now all that mattered was returning her to her rightful realm.

I was attempting to mind my manners—this was her home, after all, and her mother was a rare Elemental, but the birth of a new Unicorn was a literal miracle. One that she clearly didn't understand or appreciate.

"What's important is that she leaves with me. Immediately," I insisted, glancing around at the many eyes watching us. "She's—"

"A Unicorn," someone finally said.

A female approached wearing the traditional tight-fitting dress of the New Amethyst Coven. Bright ginger strands shimmered in a stylish ponytail and purple jewels glittered in her hair. She looked the part, with purple eyeshadow and a gorgeous necklace that marked her as one of the clan's emerging leaders. Her dress showed off her curves, as well as the floral tattoos that graced her arms.

She approached, her hands clasped, and her violet eyes went wide as she took in the gorgeous beauty I wanted to claim. I suspected violet wasn't her natural color, but the emergence as an Amethyst Coven witch would provide her with the purple magic.

A trait that ran similar to my own race, given that my eyes blazed red with my ruby power.

The female unicorn, though, her eyes shone with their natural blue. Perhaps she'd always held dormant sapphire magic, but something felt off about her.

Besides the obvious. There were no female Unicorn Shifters in existence.

And her non-unicorn mother shared her blue eyes, which suggested the female was hiding her true magical affinity.

Her father had to have been a Unicorn Shifter for this to make any sense, or some distant relative even, but this wasn't how Unicorns were typically born. I should have felt her magic at her birth.

So why now? What had changed?

Questions that needed answers.

I didn't even know her name, but that didn't matter. She belonged with me. The rest would follow.

"Yes, a Unicorn," I confirmed.

Everyone stared at me as if I was the one to have sprouted a horn.

While absolutely possible, I wasn't going to break the rules just to prove a point.

The manic laughter coming from the female's mother made me frown.

"You must be mistaken, sir. Is this some sort of joke? My daughter couldn't be something so... ridiculous."

The Amethyst Coven witch released a massive gasp in horror.

At least someone understood the gravity of the situation.

And the insult the Elemental had just spewed was to one of the most powerful supernaturals in all the realms.

"Tricia! Unicorns are legends!" The Amethyst witch snapped her fingers and a book appeared. She opened it while it hovered in midair. She flipped through the pages, giving me a chance to see her tattoos close up. I spotted insects underneath some of the florals.

Hmm, a nature witch. No wonder the Elemental doesn't like her.

The female's mother glowered at the witch, although I wasn't sure why. She was absolutely right on all accounts. "You will call me *Elemental L'Estelle* in my house, Becca."

"Mom," the female groaned. "Can you not be your usual dick self right now?" She jabbed a finger at her head. "I just sprouted a fucking *horn*."

"Watch your tone with me, Bonny Magic L'Estelle," Tricia hissed.

Bonny, I thought. *Fitting, like a little bonbon.*

Perhaps she tastes sweet like one, too...

I stiffened. The unexpected thought of *tasting* the female named Bonny most certainly was unusual, but not entirely unwelcome.

Although something else was becoming... *stiff*, a sensation I immediately knew meant arousal.

Something I was not supposed to feel unless I had abandoned my magic.

Fear spiked through me, but I forced myself to be calm. A simple test would do.

Releasing a wave of Purity magic, I watched gentle ruby sparkles drift through the air, immediately calming everyone around me, including the female who I very much wanted to *taste*.

So, I still had my magic, but I was absolutely aroused.

How is this possible?

The female relaxed as if she understood that I

would keep her safe—but with a mother like that, I mourned what kind of life she'd been subjected to up until now.

No matter. Her life was about to change.

Forever.

BONNY

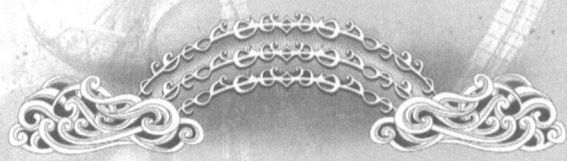

Unicorn.

Rolling the word over in my mind didn't help me process this insanity. No matter how I tried to make sense of it, it still sounded like a cosmic rainbow-colored joke.

If I turned into a supernatural, a Unicorn was definitely not the species I would have imagined, and not just because they weren't supposed to exist.

The horn on my head wasn't unpleasant, though. My headache had vanished the moment it had appeared, releasing the pressure that had been building up since the Awakening Ceremony at Fortune Academy.

This is that damn Dark Mage's fault... Professor Olivia.

I'd find her and demand her to fix this later.

Right now, I clung to the male with ruby eyes and rainbow hair.

I knew what he was.

He'd come for me because we were the same. He knew I'd awakened, somehow, and he'd come to take me away.

A life without my mother?

Maybe I should send Professor Olivia a fruit basket, instead.

Although, perhaps he was a bit too happy to see me; even though he didn't have a horn, the "horn" in his pants was certainly *large*.

It pressed against my hip, and based on the way he uncomfortably shifted his posture to try and not touch me with it, the thing was so huge that my proximity made that impossible.

Damn. Unicorns are hung—I guess that makes sense, though.

I should have given him some space, but for some reason, I didn't want to.

I enjoyed knowing that he wanted me. Dating had always been off the table for me. Witches weren't a prude species, and often encouraged early sexual experiences, but for some reason, my mother had stipulated that I remain a virgin for the indefinite future.

I'd thought about finding some random guy to throw myself at, and I'd even tried a few times to spite her, but it never panned out. Given I was a human, no one wanted me. So I'd somehow wound up becoming a nineteen-year-old virgin against all odds.

My mother frowned at us, clearly displeased with this whole thing.

"What the fuck is your problem?" I asked, finally finding the courage to push away from my Unicorn savior.

Something had come over me. My vision swam with red sparkles that set my insides on fire.

And I was *angry*.

My mother blinked at me as if I'd slapped her, her mouth popping open in stunned shock.

"Isn't this what you wanted?" I shouted, throwing my hands up in the air. "You hated me for being a human—being an *embarrassment* to your precious bloodline. And you know what? That shouldn't have been my responsibility. You could have married someone else and had more children if I was such a disappointment." I crossed my arms and glowered at her. "If you weren't such a stuck-up *bitch*, maybe someone other than Dad would have taken you."

My mother moved so fast that I didn't see it coming.

She smacked me across the face, sending my whole body lashing to the side as thunder cracked through the air.

The Coven members all around us watched in stunned shock. However, the male at my back moved to my side as his ruby eyes blazed with powerful magic.

"You will not touch her again," he warned as the air heated all around us.

I swallowed hard because *damn*, he was both gorgeous and terrifying.

Holding out a hand, I told him without words that this was my fight.

He glowered at me for a moment, clearly displeased with the situation, but finally gave me a subtle nod and backed away.

I blinked a few times. It was as if we could communicate without words. I sensed his need to defend me. The desire was almost overwhelming and I didn't understand it, but I knew these weren't my own feelings. Somehow, I was able to sense his emotions, and even though he didn't know me, he was compelled to protect me.

Finding the whole thing eerie and exciting at the same time, I turned back to my mother. Her rage was palpable, evident by the stormcloud that had formed over our heads. Tiny droplets of rain stung my shoulders and cheeks, but I raised my nose in defiance. It was the only response my mother would respect.

"Don't ever talk about your father to me," she growled. Thunder accentuated her words as lightning rolled through the ceiling. Ned summoned an umbrella for Angel—she still didn't quite have perfect control over her shifts and water often gave her a tail.

As lightning blasted through the walls, I decided that Angel turning into a mermaid was the least of my concerns. The foundation split and the whole place might have crashed down on us had another coven witch not swiftly acted.

A black-haired beauty raised her hand and chanted a spell, one that sealed the crack that had formed.

"Thank you, Ella," Becca said, then eyed us. She opened her mouth as if she wanted to say something, but instead, she turned back to her book and began desperately flipping the pages again as if looking for something that might help.

Because my mom was *pissed.*

I'd hit my mother below the belt, sure, but she was falling off her damn rocker.

"I'm never allowed to talk about him!" I shouted, apparently having lost my damn mind.

But, in my defense, I'd just sprouted a horn, so I figured I was allowed a meltdown.

Ned and Angel watched me from the stairs, their wide eyes holding a level of shock I'd never seen on their faces before—not even that time when I'd covered myself in temporary tattoos as a fashion statement.

It had taken three weeks for them to come off, too. My mother had *not* been happy and had isolated me to my room and ordered Auntie Linda to scrub me raw every night until it came off.

Now, though, this wasn't something that she could just wash away.

I felt the change all the way down to my fucking *soul.* I wasn't human anymore, and every second it felt like something was about to burst out of me.

I hiccupped at that moment, another rainbow bubble popping into the air. This time, though, it rippled with flames and burst a moment later, releasing a wave of heat.

Well, that can't be good.

"Shit," the male behind me cursed. "We need to go, Bonny. *Now.*"

Hearing him say my name sent chills down my spine.

I liked how my name rolled off his tongue with a subtle hint of desire, betraying his emotions that burned under my skin like fire.

Maybe that's why I just popped out a fire bubble.

Who fucking knows? Nothing makes sense anymore.

My mother snapped her gaze onto the male and another ripple of thunder raked through the ceiling, causing the Coven Witch named Ella to scramble to repair it.

"And what happens if I don't allow her to go with you?" my mother asked.

The male took a step forward, returning to my side, as his nostrils flared. "Then I will be forced to take her, and that would be an unpleasant outcome for everyone involved."

Take me?

Who the fuck was this guy?

She narrowed her gaze, her calculating stare

taking in his features. "You're one too," she concluded.

His nod of agreement confirmed what I had already suspected.

Although, I hadn't expected Unicorns to be male.

I don't know why I found that odd. Unicorns just seemed like pure, innocent beings of magic from what I'd read in fairytales.

Then again, unicorns are attracted to virgins, right? It would make sense if they're just all a bunch of horny perverts, wouldn't it?

Rethinking my interest in this male, I crossed my arms. "So if I'm like you, then does that make us family?"

"Not family," he said a little too quickly, turning to stare me down. "In the same way not all humans are family. I don't know your bloodline, but there are many among us, so it is extremely unlikely we're related." He hesitated, then closed his mouth.

He'd wanted to say something else, but decided not to.

The intensity of his ruby gaze made butterflies flutter in my stomach.

Secretly, I was very, very glad we weren't related. Because the urge to kiss him made my entire body ache.

It's probably just his Unicorn Magic making me want that, I surmised, trying to get a handle on my urges. *Watch yourself, Bonny.*

My little self pep talk seemed to do the trick. I shook off the strange feelings in my stomach and ignored the buildup that frightened me.

I suspected my awakening was going to come in parts, and while I'd earned a reprieve by sprouting a horn, something else was coming next.

Was I going to fall down on all fours?

Or produce a snout?

I better say my piece to mother-dearest before I lose the ability to speak at all.

"You loved Dad. That's your only redeeming quality, Mother. But now he's gone and you've made my life miserable."

I'm not sure what I'd expected to see in her eyes.

But it wasn't the glimmer of tears that formed.

"You were supposed to be an Elemental like me," she said, her words barely above a whisper. She approached, her gentle touch running down my cheek in the type of loving caress I'd never received from her before in recent memory. "You share my eyes. I always thought..." Her hand dropped and she backed away, then swiftly wiped the tears away and composed herself as she looked at my horn.

She couldn't appreciate what I was because it didn't fit in her tidy plan for me, one where I would be her little clone.

Except, the range of emotions crossing her face betrayed that she did have feelings in that broken, cold heart of hers I'd thought buried with my father.

She did love me, and now she was worried that if I was taken away, she wouldn't be able to protect me.

She didn't know anything about the Unicorns or what it meant for me to become one.

Her emotions invaded my senses like the pellets of rain dropping from the ceiling. The air burned with ruby power, as if it was acting like a conduit to allow me to feel what everyone around me was feeling.

The Coven Witches were a mixture of fascination, concern, and excitement.

A spike of excitement came from the Amethyst Coven witch named Becca. "Ah! Here it is!" She pointed at the page of the floating book as an invisible shield protected it from the rain. "Female Unicorns aren't supposed to—"

A brilliant flash of light cut her off—as did a surge of anxiety from the male who threw off his hood.

I was too distracted by his rainbow hair and the silver mark on his forehead to process what he was doing.

And whatever he was up to, it was releasing a shit ton of magic. His ruby eyes blazed as if on fire.

He snatched up the magical book from the witch, then swiped his hand through the air, releasing another flash that pushed everyone away from us on a shockwave.

Everyone except Angel and Ned. Ned had a forcefield up in preparation for the second blow, then they pushed through the crowd for me when I screamed. The Unicorn male had me in his grip as he dragged me backward.

Toward a wall of fire.

And I had a thing against being burned alive.

"Let me go!" I screamed, but he wasn't going to no matter how hard I twisted against his punishing grip.

Damn, this guy is freakishly strong for being a fru-fru Unicorn.

As if he'd heard me, his ruby eyes turned on me, burning with an intensity that shut my brain the fuck up—mostly because I forgot how to form words.

Instead, my world became raw emotion.

Rage.

Lust.

Need.

... Fear.

I blinked a few times, not sure what to do with the powerful emotions that rushed over me.

It didn't matter, because he dragged me through the fire, changing my life forever.

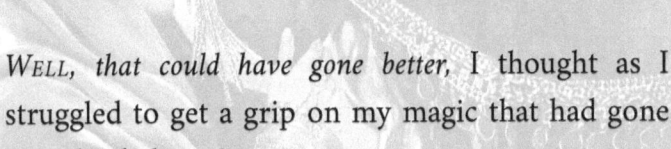

WELL, *that could have gone better,* I thought as I struggled to get a grip on my magic that had gone completely haywire.

The female at my side was responsible for that. It was as if she'd placed my soul back in my body—while setting it on fire.

A fire that burned for her.

I clutched her wrist with one hand as I dragged her onto the charred forest floor. Our entrance had been unstable, but we'd made it in one piece.

The low light turning the leaves a deep emerald glow told me it was almost dusk—the most dangerous time to be in the forest. Beasts would scent the embers burning in the dirt at our feet and come to investigate.

It wasn't the safest place to portal in, but I could sense how unstable my magic was right now. If we combusted, at least no one else would be harmed, so I'd made sure to avoid populated areas such as Starfall City or the Academy. No one would bother us here while I tried to get a handle on this mess.

Two voices proved me wrong on that count as a male and female tumbled through the flame portal, landing hard on the ground.

"Put it out!" the male shouted, rolling as his cloak rippled with fire.

The female—who had sprouted a mermaid's tail—shot water at him through her fingertips, dousing him until smoke drifted through the trees.

Fucking great.

"What were you guys thinking?!" Bonny shouted, tugging at me as she addressed the two hitchhikers. "Ned, that was reckless. I expect no less of you. But Angel, really? Walking—or, uh, *swimming*—through fire? Isn't that the one element that can kill you?"

The mermaid shrugged as her tail split back into legs. I looked up at her face as she covered herself with her hands. Like Unicorns, she was otherwise naked from her transformation.

I felt nothing in response to the woman bared before me.

Bonny, however, made my dick throb when she gave me a curious glance. Her expression immediately turned sour.

Could she be jealous?

"I had a feeling it was a portal," Angel replied, ignoring the heated exchange of emotions between Bonny and myself, "and I wasn't about to let you have all the fun without me." She winked.

I envied their easy relationship.

I'd once had a friend like that, but he was gone. Not dead—but he might as well be. Unicorns had a tough life, one not meant for a delicate, untrained female like the one who struggled against my grip.

I had to hold her with one hand because I hugged the book the witch had summoned with my other arm. It was a forbidden tome, one that had somehow found its way out of Starfall Library. I instantly knew what it was, even though my mind was not permitted to remember the events described in the book.

It might kill me to hear them.

It might have killed *her* if I had allowed the witch to read from it.

I have to get the book and the female to the Elders before this gets any worse.

"You two," I snapped, my magic still unstable,

which meant my patience was thin, "stick with me and don't stray from the path." I'd let them be devoured by roaming forest beasts in my current mood. For their sakes, I hoped they could follow basic instructions.

They looked around as confusion clouded their features. The one named Ned stood up and brushed away burnt pieces of cloth. "Path?"

Right. They wouldn't be able to see it, but Bonny might.

She turned and faced the glimmering trail of crystal dust that would lead to the Academy. Luckily, we'd landed relatively close to campus. "You don't see that?"

Angel nudged Ned. "Clothes, maybe?" she whispered.

"Oh, yeah. Sorry." He mumbled a few words and clothed her in shorts and a t-shirt. It was warm in the forest, so while appropriate wear for the temperature, it wouldn't protect her from the beasts that patrolled these parts.

While many of the creatures had learned not to venture too close to the Academy, a few would still attack if they caught us outside the campus's protection. We often permitted weaker ones to roam to deter visitors.

Except, these particular visitors I imagined Bonny would prefer to be kept alive.

"I don't see anything," Angel said as she stood and walked up to us, bravely—or stupidly—staring me down. "Except an asshole who needs to let my friend go right the fuck now."

Her words didn't affect me, but the look on Bonny's face pleaded with me to comply. Despite myself, I couldn't say no to a face like that.

I dropped her wrist, showing her that she could trust me.

The effect of ending skin contact seemed to help my magic stabilize, which confirmed that the female was messing with my powers.

Among other things, given the hard ache running through my groin and into other intimate areas.

Bonny took a few steps toward the path, then stopped and marveled at the forest.

I watched her, waiting to see what she'd do.

This place should feel different to her. And if she was as powerful as I suspected, she would recognize the sheer level of magic humming through the trees.

In fact, I had expected her to shift into her mare form the moment we'd portaled in. Any male her age would have struggled with resisting the transformation with this level of Purity magic permeating the air. The fact that she was still in her mortal body concerned me, but perhaps mares had better control over their bodies. I had no basis to understand her biology.

Fear echoed underneath the layer of defiance that made up her mixture of emotions. As a Unicorn of the Ruby House, I specialized in empathy influence, as well as the element of fire. However, the female's emotions seemed to invade my own, making me feel what she felt even when I attempted to shut her off.

When she glanced at me, her gaze flickering down to my waist where my pants did little to hide my arousal—I wondered if that connection went both ways.

Because I sensed her lust, too.

This was new and exciting for her. I felt her compatibility with Purity Magic, which likely meant she was a virgin.

Just like me.

However, if either of us acted on these urges, we'd lose our magic and ability to shift. That was a sacrifice I had never been willing to make.

It had always been that way for my kind.

Sex was the conduit for magic in other species.

For Unicorns, however, it blocked our power.

Permanently.

It wasn't that I wasn't curious or interested, but the realms were in too much danger for me to be selfish. I had a job to do—one I took extremely seriously.

Protect.

Serve.

All in secret. We didn't seek validation or glory; that would be contrary to our nature.

Unicorns had always been the invisible force that kept the realms safe from unimaginable evil.

The realms counted on Guardian Unicorns such as myself to retain their power and to keep them safe from monsters that could devour entire worlds. Monsters they never knew existed—and we liked to keep it that way.

Sexual distractions had no place in my world, aside from procreation.

I left the breeding to the Stallions.

Which meant I had no use for these strange desires. Not unless I wished to lose my identity and my ability to protect the innocent.

That was why I had separated from my soul, but this female put everything I stood for at risk by making me feel things that should be impossible in my current state.

"We need to get you to the Elders," I told her.

Her golden horn glittered under my realm's light as she tilted her head.

She's so fucking gorgeous.

Suddenly I was grateful for her friends. If we had been alone, I wasn't sure if I could be trusted around her.

Her eyes had changed color, taking on the red hue of Ruby-affiliated magic that made her look absolutely exquisite. Either she was somehow drawing my magic from me, or she belonged to the Ruby House.

As our Queen, perhaps.

I quickly shoved the errant thought out of my mind.

What was it about this female?

What power did she possess?

And why hadn't I felt her magic until now?

Questions that the Elders would have to assist me with. This was completely unprecedented and dangerous. They were much older than my mere one-thousand years. Surely they would know what to do.

"Elders," she repeated. Not a question, but a

statement. Then she laughed, the sound the most beautiful thing to have ever graced my ears. "You're telling me there's more of you? And you have *Elders?*" She propped her hands on her hips. "We're not going anywhere until you tell me where we are, and who *you* are."

"We're in the Enchanted Forest," I said easily. "My name is Raze. I'm a Unicorn of the Ruby House and, until further notice, in charge of you from here." She needed to know who she was and everything about her power if she was to control it—and she needed to know that I was her superior.

All of those things would come in time.

I had no desire to hide answers from her, but she wasn't ready for most of them.

Meaning she would have to listen to me.

It would solve all of my problems if she didn't. If a beast found us and devoured her, it would make matters a whole lot easier.

But the mere idea of anything or anyone harming a hair on her head sent fresh, protective rage through my veins.

That wasn't an option.

As if to test my resolve, a pack of bear cubs poked through the foliage.

My blood ran cold.

Like everything in this forest, creatures were deceptively adorable and boasted golden horns that held the magic of our realm.

Every creature was a containment of raw power.

Every beast was capable of ripping its prey to shreds.

In particular, Unicorn Bears. They tended to be more devastating because they traveled in family groups and the cubs were often ravenous.

We'd lost a few students to them this year already.

And like everything in the Enchanted Forest, the first step in luring its target was to appear defenseless.

"Awww, floofy!" Bonny squealed as she clapped her hands against her cheeks. "Look how sweet! Baby bear cubs!"

Their mother appeared a moment later, then rolled onto her back and showed her swollen belly.

"Bonny, don't—" my sharp tone did little to deter her as she sprinted toward the cubs.

"It's okay!" she said, already throwing herself at death's door like a naïve Unicorn foal. "You said we were in the Enchanted Forest, and look at the mom. She wants us to pet them!"

My heart dropped as she bounded across the forest floor.

Remembering how to breathe, I charged to stop her, only to ping off of an invisible wall that shimmered like rainbow oil.

Pain shot through my face and I rubbed my nose, glancing up at what could have possibly stopped me.

Not much in the realms was strong enough to contain me—except for walls of Purity magic, of course.

I blinked a few times when I realized what I was looking at.

She just summoned a level three protective barrier without even trying.

Glancing back at her, my heart stuttered as she reached one of the cubs and picked one up.

"Bonny!" I cried out, my heart already breaking even if I wasn't sure why.

I shouldn't care so much about a female I'd just met, but I found myself beating my fists against the barrier as my magic poured through me with red-hot heat.

I waited for the cub to unlock its jaw and eat her whole before I could burn my way through the barrier to save her.

The cubs were often ravenous and they traveled

in packs. The mother was actually less dangerous than her offspring and would eat what remains they left behind—if there were any.

The other two cubs at her feet sniffed her ankles, but they didn't chew off her legs with a single bite like they normally would have.

I lessened the heat running through my fingertips.

They weren't... eating her.

What the fuck is going on?

BONNY

I wasn't sure what had come over me, but the little floofy Unicorn Bears absolutely required coddling.

And kisses.

And snuggles.

I made sure to give all of the above to each little cub. Their golden horns were blunted on the ends, so I was able to nuzzle them without fear of being pricked.

Raze continued to freak the fuck out behind me, although I really didn't get what his problem was. Maybe you didn't mess with cubs in the human world, but that was because mama bears tended to be murderously protective.

This mama bear... she had *spoken* to me.

We've been waiting for you, she said. Her growly voice rolled through my mind, but I liked how it felt.

Glancing up at her, I smiled as I scratched one of the cubs behind his ears. He playfully swiped his tiny paws at me, then harmlessly gnawed on my knuckles.

The emotions continually wafting from Raze shot through me like an arrow when the cub did that.

Fucking dongbells and poisoned Skittles. How pathetic does he think I am that a little baby cub's love nip is going to hurt me?

Although for the level of panic I felt from him, I wondered why he hadn't approached by now.

Irritated at him for being such a downer, I ignored the instinct to face him and smiled at Mama Bear instead. "Is that so?"

She rolled on her back, showing her belly again. *Yes. You will save us.*

"Save you? From what?"

"Um, Bonny?" Angel asked as she approached from behind. She rested a hand on my shoulder, knelt at my side, and then leaned in to whisper in my ear. "Are you talking to the Unicorn Bear?"

Right. Talking to the animals was probably some sort of side-effect of my awakening, so Angel wouldn't be able to hear the bear's side of the conversation.

"Yes," I whispered back, "and it just got interesting."

Angel quieted, which I took as permission to let me continue. Finally.

"Guys?" Ned said, making me growl.

I was grateful for my friends who were willing to walk through fire for me, but they needed to let me do this uninterrupted.

"Not now!" I hissed, then waved for the animal to continue. "You were saying, Mama Bear?"

I expected you to know who you were, she said, her tone almost sad. She sniffed the air, directing her attention to the male behind us. *You brought one of your Vestals.*

"Vestals?" I asked.

Yes, she replied as if I should know what that meant.

The cubs rolled at my feet and nipped at my ankles, making me laugh. They pestered me until I scratched behind their ears again.

Scratches! one of the cubs demanded.

Mama Bear rolled back onto all fours and shook her head. Her ears flicked, then went flat as she turned and gazed into the forest.

We're out of time. It has found us.

Chills ran over my skin.

"*What* found us?" I asked, only for a roar to answer me a moment later.

Muffled shouts came from behind me and I whirled to find the rainbow-haired male beating his fists against a translucent wall that shimmered like oil.

What the ever-living fuck is going on?

I saw that Ned was stuck behind it too, so I approached and passed my fingers through it. It released with a soft *pop* and Raze immediately recaptured my wrist. "We're leaving, *now*."

Mama Bear growled and bounded between us and the shadow approaching through the forest.

A strange sense of emotion swept through me seeing an animal trying to protect me.

I hadn't done anything to deserve protection, yet when a massive lion with a mane of fire appeared, the bears formed a line and growled.

"This way!" Raze shouted, pulling me away from the creatures, but I stood my ground.

"No," I hissed. "I'm not going to leave them to fend for themselves. They're just little cubs!"

"You don't understand," Raze said, his ruby eyes

wild with magic and intensity. "They can take care of themselves. Let's *go*."

"Uh, Bonny?" Ned said, pointing at the beasts facing off against one another.

My eyes went wide.

The little, adorable cubs I'd called *floofs* had just turned into terrifying monsters.

Rows of teeth appeared as they unlocked their jaws and they tripled in size. Their golden horns shimmered with power, and the cubs released a horrifying roar that shook me down to my bones.

Holy fuck.

The lion charged, leaving a trail of embers in its path.

That's when the rainbow shit hit the fan and I learned why the Enchanted Forest was not a magical place of floofy cubs.

It was a terrifying place filled with carnivorous monsters.

And I was about to become lunch.

BONNY

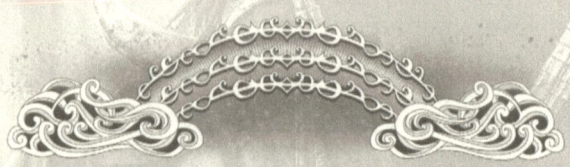

"Okay, yeah. Let's go," I finally agreed.

Because, damn. Those little cubs had just turned into forest piranhas.

Some of Raze's panic was starting to make sense to me now.

My friends nodded and we all turned to run, but a trail of fire cut off our escape route.

"Shit," Raze hissed, then whirled on the creatures. "Khimaira isn't here for them—she's here for *us*."

Khimaira.

Vestals.

My mind was already spinning trying to make sense of this place.

The lion—Khimaira—had one of the cubs in her

mouth. The little thing was doing a good job of fighting back, though, scissoring his way through the lion's maw.

Except, the plume of smoke that came from Khimaira's mouth made the cub go limp.

"Stop that, you overgrown ass-cat!" I shouted, abandoning all sense as I ripped free from Raze's grip. I didn't doubt he was strong enough to stop me, but he likely hadn't expected me to run *toward* the fire-breathing lion.

But I couldn't just abandon these animals to their deaths.

I didn't care if the cubs had sharp teeth and could change form into terrifying predators.

They didn't deserve to be cooked alive by that beast that had attacked for no reason. They were just trying to protect themselves.

Mama Bear joined me as I ran up to Khimaira.

I wasn't sure what I planned on doing, though. I didn't have any weapons, and I certainly didn't have any combat training other than the fencing classes my mom had forced me to attend.

I wasn't sure why wealthy families were so obsessed with fencing, but I was pretty good with a sword.

Then it hit me. Maybe I didn't have a sword…
not in the traditional sense.

But I did have a *horn*.

"Watch my six!" I shouted to my friends.

I wasn't even really sure what that meant. I'd just
heard it in the movies.

"I got you!" Ned shouted back, then a massive
bowling ball crashed through the trees, crushing
them.

The lion easily bounced out of the way as it
careened by.

"Really, a giant bowling ball?" Angel shouted.

Ned laughed. "Come on, that was hilarious!" He
stuck up a finger. "And, effective."

It might not have struck the beast, but it had
done its job of distracting it.

Bowing my head, I ran straight toward the lion
that was looking down the path of devastation. A
golden flash released from my body and pinpointed
through the horn, striking the creature. My strike
left a gouge along her side that forced her to release
the cub from her mouth.

It snarled and shot out a wave of fire.

I would have been burned to a crisp had Angel
not protected me with a wall of water that deflected
the worst of the heat.

"Bonny!" she shouted, panic thick in her voice.

From what I knew of her skill level, she couldn't do that many more times. She needed to be near a body of water to replenish her power, and while she was able to draw some moisture from the air, I spotted her hair already sizzling from the lion's heat.

This wasn't a fight we could win, but what choice did we have? The beast had cut off our escape route with fire.

When the smoke cleared, the lion lifted one paw and snarled at me, showing bloody teeth. It had harmed the cub, but to my relief, the bear limped back toward its mother and huddled underneath her protective shadow.

The other two cubs snarled, their horns glowing with golden, sparkling light.

I noted that the beast named Khimaria didn't have a horn. Maybe that meant she wasn't from this realm. So, what was she doing here?

Other than trying to kill us all, of course.

The lion snarled, then opened its mouth. The air shimmered from the raw heat as the creature drew in a breath.

Angel had summoned one wall of water just a moment ago. She tried to do it again, but she couldn't.

I closed my eyes, bracing myself for my short life to be over in a blaze of fire with my stomach still full of bubbles and poisoned Skittles.

RAZE

Damn female.

She'd actually wounded the legendary beast—a feat that proved to me that Bonny was special.

And that meant she needed to be protected—even the Elders wouldn't be able to argue with that now, not after what I'd just witnessed.

We needed her alive.

For once, my duty aligned with the burning desire that scoured through my heart. Even if she had been worthless to the Elders, I knew it wouldn't have changed the outcome. I couldn't let anything happen to her.

She had to be protected.

At any cost.

Rushing in front of her, I summoned a wall of

fire that rivaled Khimaira's. It wouldn't block all of the heat, but it would keep the female at my back alive.

"Raze!" she shouted as her fingers dug into the back of my robes.

I roared with pain as fire washed over me.

As a Unicorn Guardian of the Ruby House, I had been baptized by fire in my youth.

I knew what it felt like, but this was different.

Khimaira wasn't from this realm.

She was a Fate Witch's familiar, one of the lost gods and a danger to all the realms.

Because Fate Witches had all but died out, leaving powerful familiars like this one to go mad without its master.

It had been contained among the other trapped beasts of the ruins within the Enchanted Forest—so how had she gotten out?

Raw agony ripped me from my thoughts as my skin blistered, followed by the sharp sensation of claws raking across my abdomen.

I clasped one hand over my stomach and shot out the other, releasing a concentrated blast of Purity magic.

Khimaira's claws were coated with deadly

poison, but I wasn't sure how long it would take for it to have an effect on me.

Based on the burn raging through my veins, it wouldn't take long.

The lion flew backward from the cluster of glitter and rainbow crystals of my attack. Its massive body slammed into the trees and crashed through a section of forest. The dim light of dusk filtered in through the new opening, straining through the dense smoke as the ground around us burned.

My vision wavered as the beast's poison seeped through my blood.

I wasn't going to be awake for much longer.

I needed to change into my Unicorn Form.

Closing my eyes, I concentrated.

But the change didn't come.

Snapping my eyes open again, fear shot through my heart.

I hadn't lost my magic, but had I already lost my ability to shift because of my feelings for the girl?

Cursing, I used my only alternative and released the last of my magic stores. The raw power was enough to break through the fiery barrier that Khimaira had trapped us with.

It sizzled and diminished, leaving a charred exit

to the sparkling path that would lead Bonny and her friends back to the Academy.

But they had to go, now.

"Run," I choked out as I collapsed to one knee. "Run, Bonny."

Her eyes blazed with various colors, making me wonder if I was starting to hallucinate.

Especially when her hair shimmered with the same rainbow hues and her long, elegant horn glimmered with sparkling power.

So... beautiful...

That was my last thought before darkness closed in over me, and I accepted it.

Because Bonny would be safe.

ELI

WE'RE ALMOST THERE, *boys*, I mentally shot back to the squadron that would follow me through fire.

Literally.

The plume of smoke in the distance meant only one thing.

After nearly a week, we'd located the wretched beast.

Khimaira. I finally found you, girl.

Time to go back where you belong.

I was hopeful that I'd recapture the legendary beast before Raze found out about her escape.

He'd skin my ass for taking this long, and for not having answers for how she'd escaped in the first place.

One problem at a time.

Luckily, he'd been preoccupied, and the Elders had sent him off-world for some classified mission. I didn't know what he was up to, and at the moment, I didn't rightly care.

My hooves kicked up soft dirt as I galloped through the trees at full speed.

Which, for a two-hundred-thirty-year-old Unicorn Guardian such as myself, was nearly at the speed of sound.

Leaves and embers swirled in my wake and I knew that my squadron was struggling to keep up with me. While they were all graduate Guardians, most of them weren't much older than fifty years.

We'd lost too many of our kind due to recent events. Raze and I were one of the few older generational members left, aside from the Elders, of course.

As I closed in on the wall of fire surrounding the beast, I stopped short, noticing something peculiar.

Unicorn Bears faced off the creature, as did two human figures.

The latter were supernaturals, based on their auras, and they definitely shouldn't have been here.

A flash of rainbow hair through the smoky fog revealed one of our own was already in the fight.

I stopped, stunned, when I realized the limp male was Raze.

And he was gravely wounded, likely because he hadn't changed into his Unicorn Guardian form.

But why?

Another human dragged him through the break of fire.

I stared at the feminine creature covered in Raze's blood.

Wait... not human.

She boasted a golden horn, one so elegant and beautiful that it took my breath away.

Her long hair shimmered between a dull pink and a vibrant range of rainbow colors, as if her locks were confused about what color they should be.

The intense concentration of Purity magic wafting off of her left no question as to what she was, even if it was impossible.

She was a Unicorn.

BONNY

"Damn it, Raze," I cursed as I attempted to drag him to safety. "You're freaking heavy!"

Fortunately, he was unconscious, so he couldn't say something snarky back at me.

But he wasn't in good shape. Three massive claw wounds slashed through his abdomen and ran up his chest. I was covered in his blood, and what concerned me most was that his blood had started to turn black.

Like that damn lion had done something to him. Were its claws covered in poison or something?

Can this get any worse?

I didn't dare turn around to see if the lion was about to turn us into fried Unicorn crisps.

Ned and Angel worked in tandem to erect a wall

of water behind us, keeping it at bay. Angel wouldn't have been able to perform such a feat on her own, but Ned came in handy sometimes.

The bears escaped through the opening first.

Mama Bear turned and sniffed the air.

You're not ready, she lamented. Then she looked into the forest, and I followed her gaze, freezing when I spotted what she was looking at.

The most beautiful creature I had ever seen glimmered through the trees. A pristine, white coat shimmered on the Unicorn. Tufts of fur curled over its golden hooves, and a similarly golden horn arched on its forehead.

It wasn't as large as mine, but the beauty of the creature took my breath away.

Would I look like that if I shifted?

Could I shift?

I imagined myself as a horse, hoping the transformation would happen. It would be a lot easier to transport Raze's deceptively heavy body to safety if I was bigger and stronger, but nothing happened.

More Unicorns filtered through the forest and Mama Bear snorted.

They'll take over from here, she informed me, then nudged her cubs to safety. *Another one of your Vestals has come for you. You must find them all. Please... hurry.*

With that cryptic statement, she scampered off into the forest.

A roar at my back, followed by a blast of heat and my friends' screams, interrupted my thoughts.

The first Unicorn moved in a blur, slamming against the stream of fire as he used his horn to blast it away with an emerald wall of power.

Everything about the creature was stunning, even his fighting style.

He pranced to the side and wielded his horn at the lion.

A stampede made the ground tremble as an entire row of Unicorns burst through the trees. I screamed and dove over Raze as they rushed around us, kicking up dirt and leaves as they plowed past me and broke through the fiery barrier.

My skin started to tingle and burn where Raze's infected blood had touched me.

A sinking feeling warned me that I was slowly being poisoned, too, but he'd risked his life for me.

Leaving him unconscious and alone felt wrong.

Not to mention there were underlying feelings for him that I didn't understand. A need to hold him, comfort him, and kiss him back to health gnawed at me with relentless insistence.

Making out with an unconscious Unicorn

Shifter probably wasn't the best idea right now, so I glanced up to see what was happening.

A majestic scene unfolded as the group of Unicorns faced off the terrifying creature.

The lion snarled and slashed at the Unicorns, but their collective power closed it in a golden veil, trapping Khimaira.

It roared, the intense sound shaking the trees and sending a shockwave of heat blasting out in all directions that broke the golden veil, sending it shattering like glass.

My hair flew back from my face as it landed its eyes on me.

Eyes that burned with fire.

It seemed to want to say something to me, to plead with me, but I didn't know what it wished to say.

It had just been trying to kill all of us a moment ago.

But maybe the same infection that made my insides burn was making it behave this way.

Something about this felt off. I couldn't explain it.

I just knew that something wasn't right.

Then it snorted, as if frustrated, and turned.

And ran.

The first Unicorn I had seen neighed, sending the others running after it.

But he stayed behind.

And approached me as his entire body shimmered with golden power. His horn glowed with threatening heat, making me raise my nose in defiance.

Angel and Ned seemed to share my death wish, because they ran to my side and faced off the glorious creature.

"Stay back," Angel warned.

"Yeah," Ned agreed, wiggling his fingers that glimmered with purple power. "I have more bowling balls and I'm not afraid to use them."

Yep. Ned was absolutely terrifying.

The Unicorn snorted, then shifted.

Into a male.

A very gorgeous—and very *naked*—male.

I swallowed the hard lump that had formed in my throat as I openly stared at him.

He shared Raze's rainbow-colored hair, but his eyes were an incredible shade of green that reminded me of emeralds.

And his body could have been crafted from marble.

Every movement sent light rippling over pure

muscle, putting my fantasies of sparkling vampires to shame.

He might have shifted into a human form, but he was definitely hung like a horse.

His enticing gaze dropped to the unconscious male in my lap while I openly ogled him like a moron.

"What happened here?" he asked, his eyes capturing me once more. A golden light flashed in his hand as he summoned a long piece of cloth. He knelt and handed it to me. "Wrap his wounds while you talk."

It took me a few moments to find my voice. "We... were attacked," I said, doing my best to lift Raze to wrap the cloth around him. I couldn't lift him so much as roll him. I managed to loop the cloth around him a few times, then I securely tied it to stop the bleeding.

The male frowned. "I can see that. I mean, why is Raze with you and facing Khimaira alone? He knows better. Not to mention, he's supposed to be off-world." He narrowed his gaze. "This doesn't look good for you, so I suggest answering honestly."

Angel clenched her fists. "Because she's a Unicorn he was supposed to bring back here. And then some fire lion thing attacked us."

His gaze slanted to my friend. "Female Unicorns don't exist. So whoever, or *whatever*, she is, I need to know." His nostrils flared when he glanced at me again, his attention resting on the horn still glowing on my forehead. "Are you some kind of succubus? Is that how you drained his power and turned yourself into this abomination?"

Why would he think...

The way his cock began to harden answered my question.

He was attracted to me.

Fuck, am I going to have this effect on every Unicorn I meet?

Ned scoffed. "You can't trust your own eyes? Just looking at her gives you a hard-on. Do you know why that is? Because she's your species, bro. And it sounds like you don't have many females around here, so you probably have some mighty blue balls." He leaned down as if to get a better look. "It explains the crankiness."

The Unicorn stared at him, clearly unimpressed. "An erection is a perfectly normal bodily function even without sexual arousal." He sneered. "Perhaps you don't get them since you seem like a little bi—"

"You wanna see it?" Ned challenged as he

violently tugged at his belt. "I'll fucking show you who has the hardest dick you piece of—"

"Ned," I hissed. "Enough. We don't have time for this." I didn't want to get eaten alive by the fire-breathing lion just because two males were having a contest of who had the biggest cock.

And I'd seen Ned's junk plenty of times because he thought streaking was hilarious. His emotional intelligence was about that of a four-year-old, so I could certify that the Unicorn would win this one.

By a mile.

"Fine," Ned snapped as he readjusted his pants. "Then how about this?" He pointed at the book Raze had abandoned near the trees in favor of saving our lives. "That tome was summoned by a Royal Covens witch and she was about to tell us about what happened to Bonny, but Raze took it from her. Maybe you could try reading it if you don't believe us."

The male didn't seem impressed. He considered us for a moment, then finally walked over to the book and picked it up. He turned it over and hooked his thumbs on the cover, but struggled to open it.

Naturally, a good magical text would be spelled shut. So, he wasn't going to believe us until we figured out how to open it.

Not that it really mattered. I just needed to get my friends and Raze out of danger, and this forest was apparently full of it.

Although, the "completely biologically normal" anatomy of the Unicorn seemed pretty dangerous, too.

I tried not to stare, but he was just as hung as Raze, and *damn*, it was making my mouth water.

Which was not the reaction I would have expected from my libido. I typically cared more about my Amiibo collection and my signed A.J. Flowers books than I did about dick sizes.

What the fuck is wrong with me?

As if he could sense my interest, he glanced at me. His emerald eyes flickered with lust, the same kind of lust I had sensed from Raze.

He flinched and looked away, then snapped his fingers and summoned himself pants.

I was both disappointed and relieved.

"See?" Ned said. "She turns you on, right? Just admit it. Because she's a *Unicorn*."

"Or a new breed of succubus," he snarled, then approached Angel.

She propped her hands on her hips in defiance.

The Unicorn narrowed his eyes. "My squadron is going to be busy trying to recapture Khimaira. That leaves me alone with you lot, so I suggest you listen carefully and do exactly as I say if you want to stay alive."

Angel nodded. "Whatever you say, Mr. Unicorn, sir," she said in a mock voice.

I rolled my eyes. *Smooth, Angel. Piss off the powerful shifter.*

He handed her the book, choosing to ignore her bravado. "I won't be able to take this in my Unicorn Form, so hold onto it." He leaned in and showed his teeth. "If any of you try anything, I will *not* hesitate to leave you to the forest beasts. Do you understand?"

She hugged the book to her chest and nodded. "Yep. Whatever you say, horsie boy." She gave him a wide grin.

Either Angel had a crush on him, or she had a death wish.

Maybe both.

Based on the pounding of my heart, I had a crush on him, too, but maybe he was onto something with this succubus suggestion.

The way that Raze made me feel had my stomach wound into knots. Even though he was poisoned and it was making me a bit nauseous, my touch seemed to help him, so I didn't let go.

And the desire to kiss him hadn't gone away.

The only problem was that I was *also* developing feelings and desires for Emerald Eyes. That suggested something magical was going on here, giving me these feelings for not one, but two super powerful, super *hot*, Unicorn Shifters.

I didn't believe in fate. I didn't care that Fate Witches existed and that the covens believed major events were predestined.

Fate was what we made it, and so was love.

Maybe that was a human concept, but that's what I believed.

I barely knew these males, so my growing feelings for them didn't make any sense.

I didn't want to believe they were real just because magic told me so.

Magic had never done my life any favors, so I wasn't going to start trusting it now.

When the male approached me, his body began to glow. "I'll carry you and Raze to the Academy. You'll ride on my back and your friends can follow." He glanced back at them. "If they can keep up, that is. We're going to be moving fast. This area won't be safe for much longer."

"Don't you worry about us," Ned said as he wiggled his fingers. "I have just the spell..." he began chanting, but I didn't pay attention to what kind of ridiculous idea he was going to come up with next.

I was still stuck on the part where I was going to *ride* this male.

In the traditional sense, anyway.

Like, as in a horse.

My gods, my brain has gone straight in the gutter, I thought as I rubbed my temple.

Emerald-eyes grabbed my wrist, startling me. He turned my hand and frowned at the black blood that sizzled into my skin. "You've been touched by Corruption," he lamented, then looked down at Raze. "You both have."

I snatched my hand away. "I don't know what that means."

Raze stirred in my lap, then his ruby eyes blinked open. "Eli?" he croaked out.

I brushed Raze's cheek. The impulse to comfort him was too overwhelming to ignore.

He glanced up at me, then a soft smile graced his beautiful face. "Are you harmed?"

Shaking my head, I tried to pretend everything was fine. Unsuccessfully, of course, because my vision had darkened and the tingling in my arms and legs made me want to crawl out of my skin.

"You're both touched by Corruption," Eli said.

"Then leave us here," Raze immediately countered. "We can't risk—"

"No," Eli shot back. His eyes glowed with a gorgeous shade of green as his body began to transform. "You're going to the Academy."

Sparkles glimmered all around him as he burst with light, his body changing until there was that same gorgeous Unicorn standing before us.

So beautiful.

He stared at Raze, his long lashes lowering as he pawed at the dirt.

"Fine," Raze finally said, relaxing against me. "I don't have the energy to argue with you. Just... promise me we'll be isolated once we're inside. No one can come near us until it burns through... or until we're dead."

Dead?

"Excuse me?" Angel said, scampering up still holding the book.

"Nobody's dying," I assured her, even though I felt like I *was* dying.

The awkward steed that Ned had summoned trotted behind her.

A pegasus.

With bat wings.

Normally I would have laughed, but the situation was too dire for even Ned's antics to cheer me up.

Plus, I was starting to feel downright nauseated. Pain shot through my stomach and I doubled over on a groan.

Raze struggled to his feet. "We... don't have much time. The beasts will smell my blood."

Eli—now in his majestic Unicorn form—knelt on all fours and waited for us to mount him.

Raze hauled himself over the Unicorn, then held a hand out to me.

I refused it. He was injured enough as it was and looked like he was about to double over.

"Hold on tight, but try to only touch the mane and nothing else" Raze instructed as he wrapped my arms around his middle, although I was careful to avoid his wounds as best as I could. He roped Eli's mane around his wrists to secure us in place. "And use your legs. I don't know if I'll stay conscious."

I held onto him and rested my cheek against his back.

I yelped when Eli began to move and held on just as Raze instructed.

Because we were moving *fast*.

A neigh sounded as Ned and Angel followed us

on the bat-pegasus. It launched above the forest through the hole Khimaira had made.

Clever. They didn't have to move as fast if they were high up.

Ned could be smart, sometimes.

Raze groaned and leaned to the side, worrying me that he'd fall off.

"Hey," I whispered. "Stay with me, Raze."

I wasn't sure what compelled me to do it, but I pressed a kiss on his back.

He immediately jolted as a soft, white light flashed through his body.

"I'll manage," he finally responded.

I chewed my lip as I hugged his middle and watched the forest pass us by. The stabbing needles in my extremities had likewise diminished after I'd kissed him.

It wasn't gone… but it was better.

For now.

And the fact that a simple kiss had improved both of us greatly concerned me.

What kind of magic was at play here?

ELI

I was being reckless.

Dangerous.

But I couldn't abandon Raze, not after everything he'd done for me.

And despite my reservations about the female, I couldn't deny the surge of Purity magic that wafted from her.

And it was far more magic than even someone like Raze had at his disposal. My theory of a new breed of succubus was a stretch, at best, given that she seemed to be producing Purity magic on her own.

Only one creature in all the realms was capable of that: a Unicorn.

Not to mention the strange way she was making me feel.

Even in my equestrian body.

My oversized cock was doing things it shouldn't in this form, growing in size and extending from my sheath.

Luckily, none of my squadron was around to see it, or they'd be questioning my control around the female.

It didn't make sense, but the sensation of her bouncing with me as I bolted toward the Academy drew far too much of my focus. Only a thin shred of fabric separated her warm pussy from my flank. A brief, and very inappropriate, thought crossed my mind.

I wonder if this is stimulating her...

I hoped it was.

And that sudden desire to give her pleasure startled me.

I should have summoned a damn saddle, I lamented, but it was too late now.

When we ferried wounded comrades, we never used saddles. The direct contact helped us to share our Purity magic, and Raze needed all the help he could get right now. I risked myself by carrying him —and the female—since they were both touched by

Corruption.

It would burn out, eventually, but Corruption was a nasty substance with resilience that even Unicorns found difficult to manage.

Raze didn't deserve to be abandoned to fend for himself. There were too many creatures of late, and Corruption had made an unexpected reappearance. It should have been eradicated, but with the escape of Khimaira, the ancient, foul magic seemed to have returned to our forest.

Which didn't bode well for the rest of the realms if it got out.

My people's safety and the realms we protected should have been my top priority. Instead, I became more concerned with my mentor and the female who clung to him.

She was special. I knew that much, but I also didn't trust her.

Because how could I? Female Unicorns didn't exist, so what the fuck was she?

Unless… the Elders had lied to us.

Blasphemy, I chided myself. I was not one to doubt the Elders, and I wasn't going to start now.

Relief rushed through me when I spotted the oily sheen of the Academy's defense systems. It took our entire collective to maintain the massive, impenetrable bubble that kept the pristine white walls laced with vines and flowers safe.

It was attuned to our species, so I slipped through with ease.

The fact that the female didn't ping off of my back should have dismissed any doubts about what she was, but I still found her nature difficult to believe.

The irony. Many of the other races were magically influenced not to believe in Unicorns in order to keep our kind secret and safe. Was this how they felt when they caught a glimpse of one?

A horse's neigh sounded from above, along with the flapping of wings.

I glanced up to spot the warlock and his Mermaid Shifter friend on the pegasus he'd summoned.

Right, I'd have to let them in.

Pacing the path leading to the Academy's iron gates, I lowered my head and sent a streak of power from my horn.

It shot into the barrier, providing a temporary opening for the visitors to descend.

The male *whooped* as they landed. He jumped off of the creature's back and helped the female down. "That was a blast!" he said excitedly.

I snorted. This wasn't supposed to be a fun field trip for off-worlders. I was breaking a hundred rules by bringing them here, but I couldn't just leave them in the forest. No telling what kind of damage they'd do if they were infected with Corruption and traveled back to the human realm. We'd worked too hard to defeat darkness, only for it to spread again because I'd played by the rule book.

Raze had taught me that the rules existed as guidelines, and sometimes they had to be broken. It was against my nature to take matters into my own hands, but I trusted Raze.

And in this case, I knew what I had to do.

I had to protect him.

And I had to protect the female.

My heart told me what she was, even if I couldn't make logical sense of it.

She was my soulmate and Raze's soulmate, too... and this was where she belonged.

BONNY

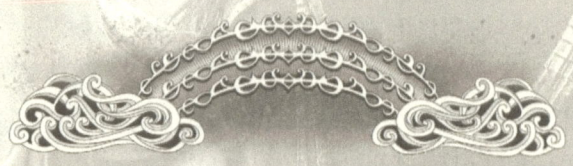

I WAS STARTING to feel dizzy, but it wasn't just because I was covered in blood, both red and black, and the lion's poison was definitely messing with my head.

It was the view.

We'd arrived at a place straight out of a fairytale. A massive bubble crested over a small city—more like a series of castles—that was surrounded by cast-iron gates. Vines grew up the sides of the pristine white walls, and the towers glistened with crystal accents.

Spires of gold pierced their air, the ends faintly glowing with power that streamed into the barrier surrounding the entire vicinity.

I could sense the intense level of magic in this

place. It made my ears hum with a faint melody I couldn't place, and my heart swelled with the feeling of goodness and the sense that I was safe.

That I was… home.

The place was clearly well protected. Given the dangerous forest surrounding us, it made sense to me that the placement had been on purpose.

What didn't make sense was how this entire world could exist and powerful supernaturals like my mother didn't even know about it.

Eli had called it an Academy, which meant this was only one small section of where the Unicorns lived.

How many are *there?*

The gates slid open and Unicorns approached in a neat line. They wore glittering golden armor and their horns glowed with power that made me both anxious and excited. I couldn't help but feel like something historic was going down.

More Unicorns in their mortal forms rode on intricate leather saddles. It would have been amusing to see Unicorns riding Unicorns, but they looked too regal for me to make fun of the situation. Their uniforms glistened with magic and their rainbow hair was strangely fitting. All of them boasted high cheekbones and breathtaking eyes.

In short, they were gorgeous.

Even Ned and Angel had been rendered speech-less. His pegasus spell wore off, the creature vanishing back to whatever realm Ned had summoned it from, and they watched with their mouths hanging open.

I didn't blame them. The Unicorns and their riders were breathtaking. The males in human forms all had rainbow hair, just like Raze and Eli, but their eyes were all different shades of gemstone colors.

Red.

Gold.

Green.

Sapphire.

Violet.

All colors of the rainbow, I realized.

And each had a silver scar marking their fore-head, leaving little guess as to their natures.

They were beautiful.

Although, their postures seemed defensive and not welcoming at all.

I couldn't blame them. Apparently, I wasn't supposed to exist.

I wasn't supposed to be here.

And I was covered in Raze's blood.

Raze wavered on Eli's back, and whatever boost of healing my kiss had given him seemed to wear off as he fell.

"Raze!" I shouted, trying to grab him, but he was too heavy. I fell with him, clinging to his robes now stiff with dried blood. The bandage I'd tied around his chest hadn't been enough to stop the bleeding.

Eli shifted into human form, then snapped his fingers to summon himself some pants before the golden flash wore off.

Apparently, he wasn't going to let me see his dick again, which was fine by me. I didn't need the distraction.

"What's the meaning of this?" one of the Unicorn males wearing a golden circlet asked as he dismounted. Unlike the others, his eyes were a bright silver, void of any noticeable color.

"Master Nox," Eli said, bowing low with respect. "I apologize for breaking the rules but—"

"Yes," the male named Master Nox snapped. His silver eyes narrowed, then shifted to me. "I'm certain I don't have to reiterate our rules or inform a general of our blessed Guardian Legion that they exist for a reason. Yet, it seems I must." His eyes glowed with warning. "We do not permit visitors, yet you have brought three." He frowned at the state of Raze's wounds. "And you have risked us all by bringing those Touched by Corruption inside the barrier."

Eli bowed lower. "I apologize, Master. I will accept the punishment you deem worthy."

Master Nox snorted. "The punishment should be death."

Eli stiffened as my heart sped up.

This was not how I had imagined Unicorns would be.

Another Unicorn Shifter dismounted his steed and approached. He rested a hand on Master Nox.

While he didn't wear a circlet that seemed to represent Nox's figure of authority, his eyes were a unique mismatch of colors, giving him his own regal flare.

The left one was blue, and the right one was green. Both irises were so exotic that I wasn't sure which one to look at.

"Perhaps we should hear him out first, brother." He glanced at me as curiosity and interest sparked in his beautiful eyes. While Master Nox hadn't reacted to me, his brother didn't seem immune to whatever attraction I inspired in his species. "Who is this creature, Eli?" he asked, directing his question to the one with emerald irises no less striking than his own.

Eli straightened. "She claims to be one of us and that Raze retrieved her from her realm to bring her here."

Master Nox remained silent for a long moment, then he approached me.

I was still tangled up with Raze trying to pull him upright, but he'd lost consciousness again.

Master Nox glowered down at me as if I was an ant that could be crushed under his boot. He watched me as I unsuccessfully tried to tug Raze up, only managing to position the male into my lap.

He continued to breathe, so at least he was alive, but I could almost feel the drain his body was taking from mine.

As if he needed my life force to survive the poison.

No… not my life.

My *magic*.

That sparked a memory, one of my mother teaching me how the flow of magic worked.

It was incredibly boring, but I'd halfway paid attention because she'd related it to science, which actually interested me.

"It's like the flow of energy—or heat, if you prefer.

Heat transfer is a magical concept that is common in the human world. Be it any type of energy—heat or magic—it will always seek a balance."

Testing the theory, I ran my fingers over Raze's cheek.

My fingertips glowed with soft, golden power, and the darkness around his eyes retreated a fraction.

And at the same time... I felt a tingling up my hand.

Looking up at Master Nox, I found him watching me with an expressionless face, but he wasn't trying to stop me.

"I need to get him inside. Food, water, antiseptic, needle and thread, and bandages," I insisted. Given my mortal status, my mother had insisted that I learn how to perform basic sutures and first aid. Lessons I was grateful for now. "I'm aware that you don't know or care about me, but Raze is important to you, right?" I'd gotten the sense that Raze had a high position among these Unicorns. And Master Nox had called Eli a general—that sounded impor- tant. If Eli had broken the rules to bring Raze and me here, then that was the thread I would pull to convince them to help.

"He is," Master Nox confirmed. "He is one of the

noblest, most powerful, and respected Unicorns among us." He rolled back his shoulders. "Which is why I know he would not condone being brought here. He respects the rules."

Eli frowned as if he wanted to say something, but luckily, the male with bi-colored eyes stepped in. "The female sounds like she knows what she's doing. It wouldn't hurt to contain them in the guest wing— it's never used, anyway."

I swallowed a chuckle at the thought of Unicorns ever having guests when they'd just explicitly stated they didn't accept visitors.

Sure, why not? They were soooo friendly.

And hot.

I bit the inside of my lip to shove out the unwelcome thought—even if it was true.

Except, I didn't feel the same attraction to Master Nox as I did his brother, Eli, and Raze.

Maybe because he'd already rubbed me the wrong way by threatening Eli's life, and not lifting a finger to help while Raze was unconscious in my lap.

A hand gripped my hip.

Oh, not fully unconscious.

Raze groaned, then nuzzled closer into my chest, practically shoving himself between my breasts.

My entire face must have blazed red because Ned laughed—loudly—only for Angel to jab him in the ribs.

Master Nox seemed fascinated by the entire situation while, at the same time, managing to look like he needed to pass gas.

That must have been his "I'll try to look friendly" face.

"Fine," he finally said, "but no one is allowed to touch them." He snapped his fingers at Eli. "Samuel will check you for Corruption, so you're to wait in the guest wing as well, but in a different room."

Eli nodded. "Of course, Master Nox."

Eli moved toward me, but then Nox held out a hand. "No one is to help them. I will not risk further contamination. We have lost too many Guardians as it is."

Eli frowned as his emerald eyes landed on me.

Then he glanced down at Raze who was practically motorboating me while snoring.

Not awkward at all. Nope.

But I kind of liked it, and the effect the vibrations had on my nipples was making the dizziness go away. Somehow, arousal seemed to be linked with burning out the poison.

Maybe that puts succubus-unicorn hybrid back on the

table.

"At least tell Samuel to bring a crystal," Eli said.

Master Nox's frown deepened—which I hadn't even realized was possible. He must have had a lot of practice tugging his lips down like that. "We don't have any that are charged."

Eli clenched his fists. "I'll charge one. Just tell him to bring it."

Master Nox sighed and looked like he was going to argue, then decided he'd had enough of all of us.

Who knows, maybe he had to get back to his butt-clenching exercises.

"Fine," he said, waving a hand, then nodded to one of the Unicorn steeds. "See that it's done."

The beautiful creature turned and galloped into the Academy. The light shimmered along his pristine coat, mesmerizing me. I stared long after he had gone, distracted only when a hand rested on my shoulder.

"I don't think you're supposed to help me," I told Angel.

She gave me a brave smirk, then glanced at the Unicorns as if daring them to try and challenge her. "They can kiss my scales. I'm not afraid of whatever black stuff is messing with you."

Master Nox snorted. "If you wish to risk yourself, that's one less *guest* for us to worry about."

By "guest" I was pretty sure he meant "prisoner."

Ignoring his not-so-subtle threat, Angel pulled me up to my feet, then glowered at Ned. "Come help, asshat," she said through clenched teeth.

Ned gaped at her and waved a hand at Master Nox. "Did you not just hear that?" Angel glared at him until he sighed. "Okay, fine. But if I turn into a frog because of some upside down Unicorn-magic-gone-wrong, you're taking care of me." He grunted as he shifted Raze's arm over his shoulder. "Flies for life, and only the best quality!"

Angel rolled her eyes, then she squeezed my hand. "Seriously, Bon, are you okay?"

I shifted under Raze's other arm and pressed a hand to his chest. His robes were so shredded that I was able to touch his skin, and right now skin-contact seemed to be the only thing keeping us stable.

Although, just the fact that it was a strange Unicorn Shifter infected with a fire-breathing lion's poison that comforted me right now just proved what kind of mess my life had quickly become.

Just a few hours ago I'd been human. Miserable, sure, but in a normal "life sucks, I'm going to be a rebel and smoke weed" kind of way.

Now?

I wasn't even sure what I was.

I had no idea if I'd ever see my mother again, which I thought I would have been happy about, but at least she was the enemy I knew.

Here, I had no idea who I could trust.

With how I reacted to these males, I felt I couldn't even trust myself.

"Totally fine," I lied, avoiding eye contact as Ned and I managed to lift Raze between us.

We slowly made our way through the open gates. The Unicorns escorted us on all sides and boxed us in, not that we had anywhere to go.

The place was enormous, as was the magical bubble that kept dangerous beasts out and us inside.

Eli closely followed us but seemed too anxious about the situation to help. At least with Ned's assistance, I was better able to manage Raze's weight. He was definitely a lot heavier than he looked.

My energy drained with every step and it felt like an eternity before we'd wound through the streets to where it was less crowded.

Males all stared at us—particularly at Angel and myself—with curious and startled looks.

It was obvious that they didn't see females very often, especially ones with golden horns.

Master Nox must have been in charge of this place because they all looked to him for leadership. He gave the Unicorns subtle nods of reassurance.

If he said anything to them, it must have been telepathically, because I didn't hear him speak. After a lifetime of growing up with witches and other supernaturals, I'd learned that just because they weren't talking didn't mean they weren't *communicating*.

Whenever he made eye contact, I sensed a wave of reassurance through the air. It felt different than a hunch, or a suspicion that there was something else going on that I couldn't see or hear in the traditional sense.

I could *feel* it.

My skin tingled and my horn hummed in response, as if it wished to resonate with the nearby use of magic.

Of course, there was magic everywhere here. It permeated the air and sank into my skin, making my heart beat faster in response.

It helped the sensation of needles that came from the dark poison digging deeper in my veins, but now my chest was starting to hurt.

My lungs constricted, threatening my ability to breathe.

I hid my condition from the others as best as I could. If the Unicorns thought I was about to keel over from this Corruption stuff, they might not allow me to stay.

Which meant I wouldn't be able to keep an eye on Raze.

And for some reason, I cared about that.

When we entered one of the buildings, I knew we were almost there, anyway. I wouldn't have to keep up the façade much longer.

"You'll watch over them," Master Nox instructed the male with bi-colored eyes.

The male glanced at me, then back to Nox. "If that is supposed to be a punishment, brother, it's not. I'll gladly stay and make sure our guests are comfortable."

"I'm pretty tired," I grumbled as I wilted under Raze's weight. "Can you show me where I can treat him?"

While I was exhausted, something inside of me couldn't let Raze die. We were connected, somehow, and I needed to understand why that was.

No, that wasn't the full truth. I didn't want to just keep him alive for answers.

I wanted him alive because of the way he'd looked at me.

As if I was the only person in the whole world.

As if everything changed the moment he met me, and now he would protect me to his dying breath.

What kind of magic made feelings that powerful?

And most important of all... Why was I starting to feel that way about him when he was a supernatural creature I barely even knew?

"Here," the male said, opening one of the doors. The inside of the chamber was immediately illuminated with a soft amber glow. Rainbow prisms broke through on the walls from the windows with the light offered by the moon's soft glow.

It was nighttime by now, although I hadn't even noticed it grow fully dark thanks to the density of the forest.

Here, though, it was as if every edge and design was intentional. Moonlight struck at the perfect angles and scattered every color imaginable across the room.

The bi-colored male ventured inside and briefly touched his forehead, which I realized was his way of releasing his magic. The slight mustiness of the room vanished, replaced by a fragrance that reminded me of citrus and melted sugar. The flavor combinations were surprisingly enticing and forced me to relax. The magical mist swept through the room, quickly stocking it with drinks, snacks, and glass bowls filled with tasty-looking treats.

"It'll hold you over until I can get you a proper meal," the male said, and I hesitantly gave him a nod of appreciation.

Ned helped me to get Raze on a bed. I sat on the edge and kept one hand on his chest. The skin contact helped reduce the pressure threatening to cut off my airway and luckily everyone else was too distracted to notice I was about to pass out.

The bi-colored male propped his hands on his hips. "I'll procure the supplies you requested; as for your friends—"

"They'll stay in a different room," Master Nox ordered from the doorway. His silver eyes glowed with soft power, daring his brother to defy him.

Angel stiffened. "I'm not letting Bonny out of my sight."

Nox snorted. "You don't have a choice, my dear, and if you think I'm going to allow three potential spies alone with one of our most valued Guardians, then you're more unintelligent than you look."

Angel didn't seem to appreciate the insult, but she let it slide right off her scales. Instead of commenting, she focused on the more important thing he'd just said.

He didn't believe our story.

"Spies?" she scoffed. "Raze is the one who came to *our* realm and dragged *my* friend into this mess. I promise you, none of us want to be here."

A loud crunch sounded from the other side of the room.

We all turned to find Ned with his cheeks stocked with sweets like a chipmunk. "What?" he asked around a mouthful of orange candy.

Okay, well *most* of us didn't want to be here.

"I'm okay, Angel, really," I told her, attempting to put as much energy into the words as possible.

She glanced at me and raised an eyebrow.

We had our own way of communicating, mostly with eyebrow-inspired expressions. No magic required.

Such as raised eyebrows and wide eyes meant *oh shit. Tell me everything right the fuck now!*

And waggling eyebrows meant *Did you guys kiss?* Which was usually an expression I gave to Angel and not the other way around.

Right now, though, I gave her the flat eyebrow stare that said *I got this. Trust me, or I'm going to hide all your salt so you can't get a saltwater bubble bath.*

She got the message.

I needed to be alone with Raze to figure this out. Everyone here was distracting me and making me question myself.

Angel rolled her eyes and marched over to Ned, smacking him upside the head. "Come on, idiot."

Everyone left the room except for the bi-colored male whose name I still hadn't learned.

He eyes me curiously, his gaze resting on the place where I still touched Raze's chest. "You're using Purity magic on him," he observed. His gaze returned to mine, holding me captive.

Fuck, he's beautiful.

"How is that possible?" he asked.

I swallowed and found that my tongue had gone dry. "I… I don't know."

He considered me for a moment, a hint of desire I'd spotted before briefly appearing before he blinked it away. "Right, well. I'll be back soon. I don't care if you're some kind of succubus, or if you're something else. Just… don't let him die. All right?"

"I won't," I said immediately.

Because I agreed with him.

It didn't matter what I was, but what did matter was Raze's life.

I just wasn't sure why.

SEBASTIAN

Fuck.

That female was dangerous. I knew that the moment I'd laid eyes on her, but the growing strength of her mysterious power only drew me to her more.

Who was she?

What was she?

Eli was clearly bent out of shape. He'd broken the rules to bring Raze back even though he'd been Corrupted. For his own protection, he'd placed himself in one of the adjacent rooms until Guille could find Samuel and bring back a crystal to begin the purge.

Even so, he'd still retreated to solitary without much fanfare.

Because he *wanted* to be alone?

I sensed based on his interest in the female that Raze wasn't the only reason he'd risked his life.

My brother wasn't known for his leniency, and if we hadn't already lost so many Unicorns to the recent resurgence of Corruption he might have followed through on ending Eli's life. He loved his rules.

What baffled me even more than my brother's mercy was his lack of reaction to the female.

Nox hadn't seemed surprised at all.

I knew Nox better than anyone, mostly because I'd spent the majority of my life trying to live up to the standard he'd set for my bloodline.

My mother was a Snow Leopard Shifter, one of the rarer shifter types in the realms, even though she'd raised us on Earth. She'd been part of the Rise and from a human lineage, so that made her new to the supernatural world. My father, of course, was a Unicorn Shifter, and he'd become a Stallion in order to treat my mother as his Broodmare.

She was a good mother, but she'd kept her distance from Nox and me because she knew what was coming.

I'd been taken at nine years old, a few years after Nox had been ripped from our mother's arms.

When they came for me, I'd been alone out in the garage fixing my bike. My mother hadn't even come out of the house.

I should have realized what would happen on my birthday. I'd actually forgotten that it was my birthday because we didn't celebrate it at home.

Thinking back, maybe it had been too hard on her to lose another son.

Or maybe she thought I wouldn't survive because of what I was. Why celebrate a birthday if it meant I was one year closer to death?

Except, I didn't die.

Even though I'd been born with bi-colored eyes, which betrayed my destiny as a hybrid. Not a hybrid in the sense of my parental lineage, but a hybrid as a Unicorn stuck between two Houses.

My soul hadn't been able to pick between the Emerald House and the Sapphire House, leaving me stranded.

Being a hybrid Guardian didn't make my life easy, and I constantly tried to prove myself. Having access to the gifts of two Houses made things more complicated. I found it difficult to master even the simplest of Purity miracles. Unicorns were some of the most powerful creatures in all the realms, and the grueling training we all were subjected to was supposed to make us stronger.

Now, I couldn't help but feel like I was failing again.

Because the female made me feel things I knew I shouldn't be able to feel unless something was very, very wrong.

My soul had been extracted the same day I'd arrived at the Enchanted Forest. That process ensured I wouldn't threaten the purity of the magic that made our species thrive. Even though there weren't any females in our realm to breed with, we occasionally had a female visitor from other realms. It was best to be safe rather than sorry.

Because with the full power of their souls, Unicorn Shifters were insatiable sexual creatures. I'd seen that from my own father. He loved my mother, but damn, I learned to knock before I entered a room.

Having my soul removed benefited our society and protected me from losing my powers.

It should have also prevented me from any sexual desire, yet its unmistakable red-hot heat coursed through my veins for the first time in my life.

I *wanted* her.

And that terrified me.

A part of me wanted to stay with her and learn more about her. She kept her hands on Raze at all times, her touch one that exuded magic and protection. I sensed her slowly burning away the Corruption that had touched them both.

The inherent intimacy of how she used the magic fascinated me.

I'd never seen anything like it.

After seeing the others to their rooms and procuring the supplies the female had asked for, I found my brother had already departed, leaving only a few Guardians behind to keep watch at the entrance and exit to the guest wing.

I dropped off the supplies, then headed out to check on Guille and Samuel. Guille had been in Unicorn form when my brother had ordered him to retrieve the crystal for Eli. Still, I could recognize any of the others no matter what form they took.

This time of night, Samuel would be studying his Sun Arts. The Sun House Guardians tended to practice after the sun had set to thoroughly test their abilities. Other realms could be in complete darkness, such as the Void, where the Dark Mages ruled, and we all had to be prepared for anything.

Shifting into Unicorn form, I galloped through the streets that I knew like the side of my horn. My hooves clapped against the smooth rock, releasing a pleasant sound as I hurried to the Sun House Training Grounds on the other side of the Command Spire.

It was always an impressive sight. Each building had a Purity Spire that fueled the protection barrier. Purity Magic consistently pushed into the sky, leaving glittering trails of power shimmering with a relaxing hum that told all of us that we were safe here.

Except the vibrations sounded strange today.

I paused, then stared up at the spot where the other Unicorns were watching.

While it was night, I should have been able to see the moon and the stars. There wasn't any forestry here to block out the view, but a darkness grew over the barrier, making the entire campus groan as if a weight had been placed on top of it.

Then a crack sounded as the barrier threatened to break.

Shit.

I wasn't imagining it.

Sprinting into a full-fledged gallop, I bolted around the Command Spire. My brother would be there, assembling the strongest among us to deal with the threat.

Since Khimaira's escape, we'd been dealing with Corruption Storms, but I'd never seen one threaten the barrier before.

Logic insisted that this had something to do with the girl, even if I didn't want to believe it.

That didn't change my plans, though. If anything, it reinforced them.

We needed charged crystals to deal with Corruption threats, and Samuel was the Guardian in command of them. Even though he was still just a student, there hadn't been anyone else to take on the role. The Sun House master had recently been killed. That left the duty to our highest ranking Sun Guardian stationed at the Academy.

Which resulted in the twenty-three-year-old being put in charge of Purity Artifacts.

Given we hadn't had to deal with Corruption for years, we were all unprepared for its sudden resurgence.

Golden-eyed Unicorns greeted me at the entrance to the Sun House Training Grounds. Each segment of the campus was designated for our distinct types of magic, the ground itself blessed with that particular brand of power. It gave

Unicorns with the same affiliation a boost. However, if the Unicorns were of different Houses, it made things more difficult.

My ears rang when I crossed the boundary, but this was where I'd find Samuel. I suspected Guille would be with him and something was preventing him from returning with the crystal we needed for Eli.

It also seemed to be the darkest area on campus, which was definitely concerning.

I shifted into human form and summoned myself some armor. Couldn't be too careful.

"Status," I ordered.

Both Guardians were in their Unicorn form, so they communicated with me telepathically.

There seems to have been a breach. We're containing it while Samuel and Guille deal with the threat.

"Alone?" I snapped.

They jolted at my tone.

I usually kept my cool, but everything about this situation concerned me.

We were following protocol, the other Guardian said. He was one of the newer students and had barely just turned twenty. *In the event of a breach, only the Legion or Master is to deal with the threat. Untrained students could only make the situation worse.*

He'd perfectly recited what my brother taught the students, so I couldn't rightly take out my irritation on him.

"Yes, that's correct." I waved a hand. "Just… give me a Sun Stone so I can stay here before I get a migraine." Just because I could tolerate the Sun form of Purity magic didn't mean it sat well with me.

One of the students shifted into human form. He didn't bother to summon clothes for himself since he would likely shift right back after he retrieved the item in question.

He ran into the small building and returned with a glowing stone on a leather strap.

Slinging the item around my neck, I relaxed as it took the brunt of the Sun Purity magic running through the ground.

I nodded my farewell. Without any time to lose, I ventured toward the growing black cloud that should have been a ball of fire.

Something had invaded Unicorn Shifter Academy.

Given my current mood, the intruder was not going to survive.

BONNY

WITH EVERYONE GONE, I was able to finally hear myself think.

I kept one hand on Raze's chest and gently stroked his skin.

"Raze?" I asked, trying to wake him up, but he didn't seem like he would become conscious again anytime soon.

His veins had turned black and spidered over his entire body, growing outward until they reached his extremities.

That can't be good.

Following my instincts, I leaned in and tried kissing him again.

Just on the cheek, I told myself, justifying it as a test for my theory.

If I were some succubus, sexual energy could be converted into magic. From what I knew of the Succubi, it had to be someone *else's* sexual energy, which made that particular breed of demons very popular at my school.

They could often be found giving head behind the bleachers, but they came with their own set of dangers. They were extremely lethal if untrained; even then, I wouldn't have wanted to be on the receiving end of one.

Except, when I kissed Raze, I was the one whose heart jumped in my chest with excitement. His warmth made my lips tingle, and it felt so *right*.

Maybe Eli was right. I was some sort of succubus hybrid, allowing me to transform any sexual energy into magic—even if the sexual energy was my own.

Forcing myself to lean away, I held my breath to see if it worked.

The darkness hallowing Raze's cheeks ebbed where my lips had touched him.

"Are you feeling that?" I asked him, but he didn't move. Instead, his body seemed intent on remembering how to breathe.

A slight wheeze sounded every time he took a breath.

I needed to do something, and I needed to do it fast.

Biting my lip, I briefly took my hand away and hurried to the desk where the bi-colored male had left the supplies.

Raze groaned from behind me, urging me to hurry. I opened the box and grabbed the surprisingly human items.

Collecting a bottle of alcohol with a white label, scissors, needle and thread, and bandages, I rushed back to Raze, only to find him doubled over as he cried out in pain.

"Raze!" I shouted, dropping everything to the floor.

His ruby eyes shot open and blazed with heat. "Kiss me," he demanded, making my eyes go wide.

Did he know what I was doing?

Perhaps. Otherwise, it was a pretty odd request to make while he was clearly dying. The dark poison had returned with a vengeance, seemingly taking advantage of my absence as it devoured his body.

The glorious light from his eyes flickered and dimmed, and I knew what I had to do.

I closed the gap between us and slammed my mouth against his.

Even though I was inexperienced, I opened for him and allowed his tongue to slip inside.

He tasted like cherries and caramel.

Mmm.

Wrapping my arms around his neck, I felt the cold poison draw into my body.

It didn't seem to impact me as much as it did him, so I deepened the kiss, breathing him in as if he was my oxygen.

He slowly went still as he fell asleep. Reluctantly, I pulled away, relieved to find him back to normal.

Yet now, I was the one in pain. I'd taken all of the poison out of him.

And put it into me.

Heat transfer, I mused as I groaned and flopped over onto the other bed.

Raze would survive.

But would I?

ELI

AFTER RETREATING to the room adjacent to Raze's, I tried to make sense of the unfamiliar feelings rolling through my body.

Sebastian had respected my unspoken desire to be alone.

And it wasn't just because I might be infected with Corruption.

The female had done something to me, although I wasn't sure what. The certainty that she was my soul mate was deeply unsettling.

Mostly because she was already clearly interested in Raze.

And the way Sebastian had looked at her assured me that if she was to be a potential Broodmare, he was going to get first dibs.

Unless we share...

I groaned as my body hardened at the thought. Rolling onto my stomach on the bed, I wished I could just fall asleep and let this crazy night pass me by.

Her intoxicating scent seemed to reach me through the walls.

Peaches and cream.

That's what I decided she smelled like. She'd ridden me bareback and there hadn't been very much separating her scent from my body.

I wanted nothing more than to knock on her door and see if she was interested in exploring this connection.

But Raze was still in there and likely deathly ill.

He would recover. I was sure of it, and despite the amount of pain I knew he must be in right now, I envied his time alone with Bonny.

Perhaps I could check on them soon...

It wouldn't be unusual for most supernaturals to share a female. Especially if it turned out that there was going to be a shift in our species and female Unicorns now existed, sharing would be the logical course of action.

Most shifter packs worked that way, from what I'd learned about them in my classes.

And I'd been a student at the Academy for over two hundred years. I'd definitely learned most of what the Academy had to offer.

Of course, I'd graduated long ago, but I'd never left the Academy. Instead, I'd decided to become a permanent Guardian and eventually worked my way up as one of the Legion's Generals.

When I'd been younger, my drive had been to change the Unicorn laws for my mother's sake. She didn't even know I was alive.

Now, though, I'd grown out of that.

Or perhaps I'd given up.

I was actually even older than Master Nox, but I didn't have the drive for his position.

I was content.

Or at least, I used to be.

Before... her.

Now all I wanted to do was to bury my nose in her neck, then run my tongue down her...

Stopping myself before the thoughts ventured too far, I remembered why I wasn't supposed to be feeling this way.

If I did give in, I would become a Stallion.

I'd lose everything. All my years investing in learning how to be the perfect Guardian would be thrown away.

But would that be so bad? Perhaps this would be my reward after all I'd been through.

I'd seen death and suffering.

I'd faced countless enemies.

What if this was my time to find joy?

And if she was a Unicorn, would the exchange of magic still work that way? Perhaps she marked a change in our species.

An evolution.

I knew it was naïve to think that I could have a Broodmare and keep my powers as a Unicorn Shifter, but I was already fantasizing. As long as I didn't leave this room, it wasn't going to hurt anything.

Burying my face into the pillow, I groaned as a new rush of lust hit me.

I wasn't used to the sensation, and I suspected that this powerful wave of need wasn't coming from me.

But from Bonny.

She was in the other room, and Raze wasn't awake.

He was stable; I sensed that much.

But she was in pain.

I wasn't an empath, so I wasn't sure how I could be so certain about that. Empathic abilities were known to the Ruby House, not something a Unicorn of the Emerald House should be able to experience.

But the fact that I could sense her state and Raze's suggested there was already a connection between the three of us.

Sitting up, I frowned when I sensed something new.

The ground trembled and then an icy sensation ran up my spine.

The pain hit me a moment later.

Hissing in a cold breath, I struggled off the bed and pressed my palms against the tile.

I wanted to touch the soil of my realm. My Emerald Purity magic was strongest through nature and could be a healing force.

Although I'd never tested it against Corruption inside my own body before.

The cold feeling that progressed through my veins told me the worst had come to pass.

I'd been infected by Corruption.

And unlike Raze, I didn't have any experience on how to fight it.

MASTER NOX

"Lock it down," I growled at the pitiful number of Guardians that surrounded me.

We'd lost too many.

I wouldn't allow us to lose any more.

Eli's Legion was off chasing Khimaira, and clearly, they had failed because this was an all-out resurgence of Corruption within our realm.

Something that should have been eradicated a long time ago.

"Sir," a student with blue eyes said before scampering off.

I supplied orders to the others, mostly because I needed them busy and distracted while I dealt with the Elders.

If only the Elders believed in me like my students did.

Their eagerness reminded me of my brother— when he'd once respected me.

We'd only been children back then. Innocent and blissfully unaware of the weight of responsibility that would be on our shoulders.

Sebastian resented me for many reasons and because I'd walled myself off from him long ago.

I had my secrets, secrets that could never be revealed.

That was the burden I bore to ensure he and the others of my kind were safe.

The appearance of the female threatened every-thing—but it also provided an opportunity.

I had my suspicions that Unicorn Shifters could mate without losing our powers. Our kind would be unstoppable if we didn't have to rip out our souls and live half-lives just for the sake of our Purity magic.

There had to be a better way.

And the female could be the key to everything I had been trying to achieve for over a century.

Raze was ten times my senior, and he wasn't Master of the Academy—or even something greater —because he preferred working on his own.

He rejected recognition of any sort.

Even after his involvement with Calamity.

But he was still the most ancient and powerful Unicorn Shifter among us, aside from the Elders, meaning he was the perfect candidate to test my theory.

Yet I wasn't the only one interested in the female's power. The forest had come alive when Raze brought her to our realm. I'd felt the shift in the forest's magic like a shockwave, and I felt the change still going on.

She disrupted the balance by merely existing.

Which meant that Calamity would want her.

Calamity—a force dealt with long ago, could never be truly extinguished.

That's why it had once been contained in the Ruins.

Calamity was chaos, death, and darkness.

It thrived on imbalance, and it had left a little gift for us that kept on giving.

Corruption.

That female had brought it into my home, but that was precisely how I would keep her a secret.

I did love my secrets, after all.

Stepping onto the communication platform, I activated the crystals with a single thought.

While in human form, I didn't have a horn. Still, I felt the phantom surge of power across the scar on my forehead as Purity magic from all the Unicorn Houses ran through my veins.

I stood at the top Command Spire where windows on all sides allowed me to see through to the training grounds.

Each held a Containment Crystal continually fueled by the students of each House. It made the Academy vital for our continued survival because it wasn't just a place where our youngest among us were trained.

It was where the strongest among us gave everything they had to ensure the rest of us survived.

And the Academy served as a place to protect that which gave us our power.

But the system only worked when all of the Houses contributed equally.

Frowning, I noticed that the Sun crystal seemed to be malfunctioning. A dark shadow hid that part of the campus from me, but I'd spotted my brother heading that way. He'd take care of any disturbances and remedy the situation soon enough.

He and I didn't always see eye-to-eye, but I knew I could count on him when it mattered.

"I take it you do not have good news for us," a

voice boomed, redirecting my attention to the holo-gram of a male with a long white scar on his forehead.

He didn't look older than thirty, like most immortal supernaturals, but I wasn't fooled by his youthful appearance.

He was as ancient as time.

I didn't answer him immediately, primarily because I was considering my response. Belial wasn't the most dangerous of the Elders, but he was a close second. He had once been a demon but found a way to slide his moral scale and redeem his soul.

It had changed him into a Unicorn—a creature of raw magic and perfect power.

That was the extent I understood of his history. For all I knew, he was one of the first Unicorns to exist and a founder of one of the Houses, but it was impossible to know which.

The Elders only wanted us to know that they were beings of raw power.

It was probably everything someone like Belial had sought for. I didn't believe for a moment that he had become a Unicorn Shifter out of the goodness of his heart.

No, his interests were in power, control, and most of all, Calamity.

He was the reason we had a collection of creatures locked in the ruins. He had been the most outraged among the Elders to learn of Khimaira's escape.

Losing one of his pets was indeed an absolute travesty.

I didn't bother informing the Elder of the losses we'd sustained thus far. "We have located Khimaira," I told him, knowing that's what he would be most interested in.

His black eyes sparkled with interest.

It was always eerie to converse with an Elder directly like this. While my eyes had turned silver by my acceptance as a Conduit of the Houses, prolonged exposure to every brand of magic the Unicorns controlled eventually burned out one's soul.

Evident by the dark, soulless eyes that stared back at me.

Demons didn't have souls, not exactly, so I supposed that Belial never had a soul in the first place. Or maybe he earned himself one early on in his transformation, only to ironically lose it again.

While an interesting quandary, I had more important problems to focus on.

Such as the matter of my own survival.

Because if any of the Elders ever discovered that I was lying to them, they'd rip my horn from my head and let me bleed out to death.

"Go on," he pressed, not trying to look too eager, but the way he ran his fingers through his hair gave him away.

He once had horns, so the rumor went, and he often subconsciously tried to feel for them when he was anxious.

I imagined it was similar to how I felt in human form without my horn. It was as if a vital piece of me was missing, and I didn't care for it.

"The Legion is tracking her now," I told him. Since I would require more updates from Eli and Raze, there honestly wasn't more to say on the matter than that.

"Hmm," he said, nodding. "I expect an update by nightfall tomorrow."

"Of course, Elder Belial."

He paced the length of the chamber, his gaze going out my window.

Even as a hologram, the connection was still

magical, so in many ways, it was as if he was right here with me.

Luckily he wasn't *actually* here, or else the sheer power of his magical aura could have rendered me unconscious. The Elders resided in Starfall City, separated from the rest of our society for good reason. They'd absorbed too much magic over their millennia of years, making them walking conduits of power that could often cause more damage than good.

It was a lesson for us all that more power wasn't always the answer.

Sometimes the answer rested on how to let power go.

"What has transpired?" he asked, pointing at the dark spot on campus.

I pretended to seem distraught that he'd noticed when in reality, he was falling right into my plan.

"A minor breach."

He whirled on me, his dark eyes sparking with a surge of power. A hum of energy escaped the hologram, making me grab my chest as the pain hit me like a spear.

"Only one thing could cause a breach," he growled. He approached me, making every hair along my arms stand on end and the sensation of fire run up my spine. "Are you telling me that you've failed to contain the Corruption released by Khimaira's escape?"

He didn't care about the Guardians or students we would lose—nor the ones we'd already lost. That was the dark secret about some of the Elders that I had to keep, or it would destroy morale.

Fortunately, not all Elders were like Belial—but how such an impure creature could be the embodiment of Purity magic fascinated me.

Because magic required balance.

And in order for Unicorns to be Pure, a few among us had to be impure.

Which meant his rage stemmed from selfish reasoning. He had other treasures hiding underneath the Academy's protection that he cared about.

I took my time answering him. Belial knew that I carefully considered my responses, which was something he liked about me.

He also knew I liked my theories and plots, which was exactly why I had to give him this distraction so he wouldn't pick up on the other little secret currently safely tucked away in the Guest Wing.

"We are charging new Containment Crystals to

manage the situation as we speak," I told him as my throat constricted.

His nostrils flared until his invasive magic finally retreated. "See that you do, Master Nox, or I will convince the others that it's time to force Raze into your position whether he wants it or not."

Assuming Raze survives the night, I mused, but luckily I had stringent control over my tongue, and the words didn't slip out.

"Of course, Elder Belial."

Satisfied, he dismissed the connection and his image dimmed. The room grew dark as the crystal platform shut down, leaving me with a view of the Sun House Training Grounds that were still dark.

Don't let me down, brother.

I'm counting on you more than you know.

BONNY

Something was wrong.

A part of me wanted to check on Eli, although I wasn't exactly sure where he was.

Somewhere close, I decided, *and distressed.*

Probably because he hates me.

I groaned as pain lanced through me, shoving out any concerns for Eli's opinion of me.

I had my own problems to deal with, like the debilitating poison that I'd pulled from Raze's body.

Clenching my fingers into the bedsheets, I turned and tried to bury my face into a pillow, but my horn caught the side of the bed and ripped it.

Right. Can't sleep on my face.

The other males didn't have horns in their

human form, but they also didn't have vaginas. So, I didn't think they'd be a good basis for understanding my biology now that I was a Unicorn Shifter.

Maybe it's permanent?

Pain raked through me, a cold sensation gripping my heart and sending me flinging onto my back.

"Fuck," I ground out.

Glancing over to Raze, I was glad to see that I'd taken all of the dark poison out of him, but it was doing a number on me.

However, just looking at him gave me a small measure of reprieve.

Heat transfer, I reminded myself as pain laced red lines through my vision.

Digging my fingers into the sheets again, I groaned and writhed as I tried to escape the pain.

The answer to my problems ran with a new ache through my core.

I had to get rid of this dark energy inside of me.

And the only way I seemed to be able to relocate it was through sensual acts.

Testing my theory, I slipped my fingers under the tight waistline of my skirt. Relief washed through me the moment I grazed myself.

Oh...

I'd used toys and pleasured myself before, but this time felt different.

Glancing at Raze, I watched his chest's slow rise and fall. After everything he'd been through, I expected him to sleep through the night.

The dim lights in the room made it easy enough to see me if he did happen to open his eyes, so I waited a moment to make sure he was asleep.

Satisfied, I closed my eyes.

And began again.

Normally I had to concentrate to reach climax, but this time it was as if my body craved the magic that the sexual energy released. I listened to my instincts, and it didn't take long before I was close to ridding myself of the Corruption that burned in my veins.

I wasn't sure where it would go, but I didn't really care. I wanted it out of me.

Yet, when I reached the cliff, I couldn't quite tip over. It was as if something important was missing from allowing me to climax.

Growling with frustration, I spread my legs and inched my skirt a little higher, about to take off my underwear when the weight on the bed shifted.

My eyes flashed open the moment Raze slipped between my thighs.

And ran his tongue over me, incinerating the fabric right off my body with his unique magic.

I screamed when the pleasure hit me.

And that's when I fell apart.

RAZE

FOR THE FIRST time in my life, I'd just made a female come.

On my tongue.

And the taste made me delirious.

Like cotton candy, I mused. The female that undoubtedly was my mate would taste especially sweet.

Because I was a Unicorn Shifter, her Stallion, and with a name

like Bonny, she was a treat I wanted to devour over and over again.

Her brilliant blue eyes glittered with tears. Tears I'd brought her to with pleasure.

I'd made her scream.

I wanted to hear that delicious sound again.

"Raze," she pleaded when I lowered myself over her hips, taking my time to drag my tongue over her. She stiffened when I reached the swollen nub that tasted like a cherry lollipop. I licked it, then sucked it into my mouth.

She had a neat little line of hair that ran over her mound, directing me to the tasty treat.

She bucked off the bed and I held her hips down. I wasn't done with her yet.

"Just one more," I begged her, my words muffled by her body as I sank my teeth gently into her.

She hissed, a sound that could have been pain or pleasure.

Then she moaned.

Oh, more of that, please.

She ran her fingers through my rainbow hair as if to encourage me.

Then she tugged, violently, pulling me closer to her.

I liked this possessive side of her.

This need that thrummed between us both.

My dick ached to be inside her, but she was a virgin.

As was I.

It didn't matter that I was a thousand years old.

To any other race, such a long life without intimacy would be horrific.

Unicorn Shifters were different. We didn't mate unless we had chosen the life of a Stallion. I had allowed any sexual desire to be stripped from my soul.

Yet, somehow, this gorgeous creature had put it back where it was supposed to be.

Because I wanted her more than anything.

I'd enjoyed my life as a Guardian. Or, at least, I thought that I had.

My life held purpose.

But it was a purpose that the elders had assigned to me.

Now I had a new one. I existed only to worship her.

Bonny.

Instead of being the Guardian of the Realms, I would be hers alone. I would protect her to my dying breath.

And every chance I got... I'd make her scream for me again.

"One more," I begged her again, rolling my tongue over the place that tasted sweetest. Perhaps I didn't know what I was doing, but I paid close attention to how her body moved. "I just need one more."

I licked a little higher.

Her grip tightened.

"Yes," she agreed, awarding me for doing it better this time.

I loved this kind of lesson. I would spend my entire learning her body, and her soul, in every way possible.

I wanted to please her.

To make her scream my name again.

As her entire body tensed, I tried something new.

I pulled away.

She growled with warning, but the flushed features of her face told me I'd just done something correctly.

"Raze," she warned.

I grinned, then teased her, running my tongue around the place

that had made her tighten like that.

She squirmed and whimpered, but I sensed a different sort of

build.

One that would be even more rewarding than the last.

I might be new to this, to *her*, but I was a quick learner.

I planted kisses all over, never quite touching the place she seemed to want me to go so badly.

Her aroma made my entire body tighten. The scent of melted sugar and strawberries surrounded me, something I'd only heard about from other Stallions.

It was a sign of a fertile Broodmare.

Tucking that bit of information away, I waited until her gorgeous blue eyes glistened with tears again.

I wasn't going to make her beg. I only wanted to give her everything she needed from me.

And right now, she needed me to finish what I'd started.

So I closed my mouth over that delicious little cherry of hers.

And I sucked.

Hard.

So fucking beautiful.

Bonny arched her back as my flames licked over her, devouring the fabric that hid her from me.

Until nothing was left, leaving her naked for me to appreciate.

To worship.

Her need had woken me from a feverish slumber.

Her kiss had healed me from Corruption, which had told me everything I needed to know.

She was Purity incarnate, and she was perfection.

I didn't understand how this was possible or why the Elders hadn't ever spoken of such a creature. Whatever Bonny was, she'd shifted my entire world.

And now that I'd tasted her... I wanted more.

Delicious, I decided as I ran my tongue over her again.

She shivered as she came down from her high, but I wanted to make her scream like that again.

Unfortunately, I hadn't considered that we weren't exactly alone, and the door slammed open.

"Bonny!" her friend, Angel, cried. "I heard you scre—" Her words were cut short when the lights reacted to her presence and illuminated our compromised position. These really had once been guest chambers integrated with every comfort and amenity, and a visitor entering the room would trigger the automatic lights.

Which meant that Angel could see everything.

Bonny tried to squeeze her legs closed as she panicked, but I was in the way. Instead, the motion shoved me onto her beautiful, swollen flesh.

I couldn't resist, I ran my tongue over her again.

Angel had chosen to intrude, so I wasn't going to stop my worship for her sake.

"Raze!" Bonny cried, but the effect of my tongue on her made her back arch as a wave of her magic mixed with mine.

Now with the lights on higher intensity, I could see the dark shadows that pebbled on her skin, only to evaporate from the heat of my Ruby purge.

My fiery magic hadn't just burned off her clothes.

It had also helped her purify her body, ridding herself of the Corruption that poisoned her veins.

We'd never been able to combat Corruption in this manner. It took a powerful amplification of our powers through artifacts and crystals to have any effect on the ancient evil.

It was infectious and resilient.

Yet, the combination of my Ruby prowess with Bonny's brand of Purity Magic had a potent effect.

One that could change everything.

You're the answer to everything, I decided.

"A gift," I whispered against her warm flesh, then thrust my tongue inside her.

Her body reacted as she gave in and spread her legs, allowing me more access to her. Her fingers curled into the bedsheets, but not in pain.

"More of that," she ordered.

I obliged. She tasted like cotton candy, strawberries, and addiction.

I had a feeling that after tonight I'd never get enough of her.

"I'll... leave you two alone," a voice murmured. Then the door slammed shut, indicating that Angel had left us to our passion.

When Bonny came undone again, I watched the last of the darkness leave her body. It withered into the air until only sweat glistened on her skin.

The intense need to make her orgasm ebbed, and my sanity seemed to return to me.

I blinked a few times, then sat up, feeling a bit dazed.

Then I looked down at the gorgeous, naked female beneath me.

And I realized what I'd just done.

Fuck.

BONNY

My ENTIRE BODY sang with pleasure and pain.

Pain because whatever Raze had just done to me had forced the Corruption out of my body. It had left me feeling weak and exhausted.

And starving.

But I couldn't do anything but lay there as I gulped in lungfuls of air. I'd never come that hard in my entire life.

Twice.

And now that it was over, I realized that we'd both been influenced by something magical.

Something more powerful than either of us could understand.

He seemed to come out of a daze as he finally averted his eyes. "Are you okay?" he asked.

I found the question sweet.

While I was a virgin, he hadn't done anything that had been painful. The only thing that had actually hurt was where the Corruption had left my body. My skin tingled and burned from the lasting effect.

My pride had also taken a slight hit, as well.

Because I'd just spread my legs for a complete stranger.

"I'm... confused," I admitted as I drew the bedding over my body. I shimmied up against the headboard and wrapped it around my chest, then I balled my hair up at my neck to cool off. The crisp air felt amazing against my skin.

Raze's ruby eyes had shifted to my exposed neck, then he seemed to catch himself as he cleared his throat and shifted off the bed. "I owe you an apology, Bonny. I'm not sure what came over me."

"No need to apologize," I said as I rested my head back against the headboard. It kept my hair in place so I could wrap my arms around my body. "Clearly, something magical just possessed both of us." I'd been around enough supernaturals to see a thing or two.

Including orgies.

My mother wasn't a prude. She'd hosted a few

herself and allowed me to watch, although I'd had a bodyguard to ensure that's all that I did.

I found it more fascinating than anything.

Sex that involved magic seemed to defy physics, and I'd always wanted to know more about how it worked. I didn't believe that the simple act of placing stick A inside hole B was enough to produce any sort of special power.

Yet, whatever I had just experienced with Raze proved that I'd been looking at the process all wrong.

"So you're not mad?" he asked. He didn't look at me when he spoke. Instead, he ran his fingers over the table of candies that Eli had summoned. He'd mentioned something about an actual meal, but no one else had come to check in on us, so he must have gotten held up.

Based on what had just transpired, I was glad that no one had actually seen—

I gasped as the memory of the door opening hit me. "Angel!" I shouted as I covered my mouth with a hand. I'd been so wrapped up in the moment that I hadn't even been able to stop Raze while she was watching.

She probably thought I'd lost my damn mind.

Maybe I have, I mused.

"Do you think she's angry with me?" he asked.

"Probably," I said, letting my hand drop to my side while I held the blanket up with the other. "She knows I wouldn't just do that with anyone, especially when I've never—"

I immediately shut my mouth when I realized I'd said too much, but it was too late.

Raze smirked at me. "So you're a virgin then?"

I chewed my lip as I debated how to reply. It wasn't really any of his business, but that wasn't really why I didn't want him to know.

I was embarrassed.

He was so fucking gorgeous and clearly older than me.

Likely a lot older.

He'd probably been with millions of girls. What could I possibly be to him? Especially when all I'd done was take. The magic had been one-sided, for the most part. I'd only needed a kiss to take the Corruption out of him. But to burn it out of me, I'd needed not one but *two* orgasms.

From his tongue.

My entire body shivered at the delicious memory before I quickly locked it away.

It was too late. He walked over with a tray of savory food that made my mouth water. He must have used some of the surplus of his magic to create an appropriate meal rather than expecting me to sustain myself with treats.

"It's okay," he said, lifting one of the little sand-wiches to my mouth. He persisted until I took a bite.

While I chewed, he added, "I'm a virgin, too."

SAMUEL

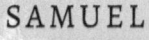

"IT'S THIS WAY," I hissed as I peered around a corner wall.

I didn't bother using telepathic communication with Guille. His powers were far too unstable for that right now. At only nineteen, he was easily overwhelmed by magic.

My eyes struggled to adjust to the darkness that pressed in all around us. But, at least I could still see.

The faint outline of the red stones that should have been burning hot with Sun House Purity magic could barely emit even a pitiful glow.

The ground, too, should have been molten embers. Instead, smoke sizzled up into a dark sky and disappeared into nothingness.

No stars.

No moon.

Just a dense fog that threatened to suffocate me.

Taking in a deep breath, I resisted the urge to turn back. Even though breathing was becoming more difficult, we couldn't stop now.

I squinted and willed my magic to pour over my vision, giving me just enough light to make out the next row of stones.

It was a skill I'd mastered in the past year. I'd passed three full years of Sun House training that made facing Corruption somewhat manageable.

Unlike my Lieutenant, Guille, who pressed in at my back and blindly groped for me. He was the youngest member of the Legion in our history, but he hadn't mastered even the simplest of skills that would give him an edge. His power was raw and untrained, so I needed to ensure he stayed behind me. "Where? I can't see a damn thing," he complained.

I batted his hands away. "Use your other senses like Professor Soleil taught you," I grumbled back at him before I bolted to the next stone wall.

The Sun House Training Grounds consisted of a series of maze-like structures that normally would work in favor of our gifts. We would practice on

UNICORN SHIFTER ACADEMY: BOOK 1

moving targets and blast them with Sun House Purity magic.

Now, though, the walls only made it more difficult to see where I was going, even if they did provide shelter.

I didn't like the tension or the wait.

Professor Soleil would probably have scolded me for my lack of patience, but there was a reason I was in charge of the Purity Artifacts.

I was hot-headed, impatient, and above all, stubborn as fuck.

That made me a powerful adversary.

Ironically, it made me very good at purifying Corruption, as well.

"How do you know we're going the right way?" Guille asked as stone crunched under his feet in his attempt to follow me. He slammed into the wall at my left and ground out a curse.

I rolled my eyes. "Because it's darker this way," I whisper-yelled. "And can you stop being such a Unicorn elephant? This'll be a lot easier if we take the bastard by surprise."

Something had intruded on campus and blotted out the power of the Sun House.

Meaning, whatever it was, it had to be intensely powerful.

171

I probably should have waited for someone higher up in the Legion to find us, but there wasn't time. Corruption was good at two things.

Killing.

And *spreading*.

I knew better than anyone that Corruption had to be stopped at the source or else we'd risk losing the entire Academy. Guille, despite his inexperience, was more powerful than me and Professor Soleil put together.

Plus, I liked it here. Unicorns like Professor Soleil had taught me how to channel my anger into something useful. I had a purpose here, and I cared about students like Guille.

I hadn't been able to save my bond brother, my family, or the members of the Legion who had tried to save me just three years ago.

A similar experience had befallen Guille. The only difference was that he'd vanquished the monster that had wronged him.

I'd failed in that regard.

"There," I said as I crouched.

One of the spots at the end of the training yard sank into a deep abyss.

That's where the Corruption would be waiting.

"What's it doing?" Guille asked as he leaned uncomfortably close to my ear.

I pushed him away. "It's feeding."

This area should have been blazing with light. Instead, the Corruption was sucking it in and devouring it.

I'd never seen Corruption behave this way before. Something was different.

Which meant something was very wrong.

"Maybe we should wait—"

I didn't allow Guille to stop me from charging forward. Now that I knew where the bastard was waiting, I planned on taking it by surprise.

Rushing forward, I stealthily crossed the distance as I shifted. My body reworked itself into my equestrian form in a few calculated moments. I was quieter in human form but more powerful in my Unicorn one. I'd learned to shift on the move, something that Guille would not have yet mastered.

I reached the black abyss the moment my hooves slammed against the broken ground, announcing my presence when it would be too late for my adversary.

I lowered my head, aiming my horn for its center. There was a creature somewhere inside the darkness. I'd aimed directly for the middle. With my momentum, it wouldn't stand a chance.

A face appeared once I had been fully engulfed in the darkness.

Golden eyes stared at me with blind hatred, and a familiar golden tattoo ran around a male's collarbone.

I couldn't stop in time when I recognized Professor Soleil.

My horn penetrated straight through his chest, and darkness spilled out all around me.

The Corruption wasn't just a monster.

It had infected my Professor.

And I'd just killed him.

SEBASTIAN

A FEW MOMENTS EARLIER...

It was proving more difficult to locate the breach's source than I'd anticipated. The Corruption Storm had never been this dense before.

Then again, we'd never had a breach before.

In my one hundred and fifty years, I'd never seen the heart of my kind threatened in this manner. The closest thing had been Calamity, but that had been primarily focused on other realms. We fought battles of our own choosing.

This time, the monster had sought us out.

I doubted it was a coincidence that Corruption had breached the barrier while the rogue female had been brought inside.

Was she some sort of spy?

Or was she our savior?

My intense attraction to her and my desire to protect her suggested some strange sort of magic was at play.

I didn't like to be influenced or controlled.

Shrugging off the strange feelings, I paused when I picked up the faint sound of human boots crunching on gravel.

"Guille," I whispered to myself. He was the only one powerful and inexperienced enough to be lingering around in the heart of a Corruption Storm while at the same time tromping around like a Unicorn Elephant.

I chuckled when I overheard Samuel in the distance calling him exactly that.

My hearing was exceptional, but depending on the nature of the Corruption around us, if I could hear the two young students, then the threat would know they were here, too.

I wasn't sure what form the Corruption would have taken this time, but I suspected it wasn't like the instances I'd come across before.

In the past, it had taken the form of a forest creature.

At least, that's what my brother had tried to convince me of.

My suspicion? It took on an actual host, and the creatures I had killed thus far had once been native to the Enchanted Forest.

A chill ran up my spine—which was an odd feeling when I was walking on the Sun House Training Grounds. The faint layer of heat that ran underneath the gravel all but dissipated, leaving only the icy darkness of Corruption that pressed in all around me.

I debated shifting into Unicorn form, but like most of my kind, I couldn't travel as quietly when I weighed over two boulders, or over one-thousand pounds in earth units—the United States, specifically. After my time during Lucifer's uprise, I'd been around humans long enough to learn their overly complicated metrics.

I also understood why Samuel spoke aloud to Guille instead of communicating telepathically. Guille was one of our youngest students.

But I knew not to underestimate him. I'd seen what he was capable of.

Adrenaline spiked through my veins when I heard the distinct impact of hooves on gravel.

I bolted into action, bursting into a shift in a single moment that I'd mastered after the past century of practice.

The magicked leather around my neck stretched to accommodate my Unicorn form, and the Sun Stone blazed over my chest. It reacted to the Purity magic that I released in a wave.

The blast of light revealed a gruesome scene of Samuel and his intended target.

I stopped short, realizing that the Corruption had either taken on a strikingly similar form to Professor Soleil...

Or it had infected him.

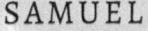

SAMUEL

"SAMUEL!" Guille shouted.

He ran up to me with his hands on fire. His raw power raked through him unchecked, which would have been terrifying on anyone else.

Purity magic tended to be *consuming*.

His body handled it, though. He was one of the few among us who was just as powerful in human form as his Unicorn one. He seemed to prefer remaining on two feet. And it wasn't to show off.

I watched in awe as he launched his magic into the air, sending it crackling against the Corruption.

The reason he remained human was so he could do *that*.

Which was probably why he hadn't mastered basic skills like telepathic communication yet.

Professor Soleil grunted in pain and wrapped his fingers around my horn as the darkness around us threatened to implode. His touch should have been blazing hot.

Instead, it was as if he was made of ice.

Intensely repulsed by the sensation, I shifted back to a human.

It was the easiest way to dislodge my horn from his body and begin healing him.

Except, the moment I shifted, Professor Soleil opened his mouth and roared. His jaw unhinged from his mouth, stretching abnormally as the horrid sound felt as if it was clawing its way through my skull.

I'd never heard such a sound in all my life. Throwing my hands over my ears, I tried to hide from the agony that raked through my body.

Something was terribly wrong.

This wasn't Professor Soleil. Or at least, this wasn't the Professor I'd known since my admission to the Academy.

Black blood oozed from the hole in his chest where my horn had been.

The Corruption is in his bloodstream. Not good.

And it was doing something to him.

He should have been dead. Instead, a light blue tint seemed to strap his spirit to his body. It wasn't the Corruption's effects that were keeping him alive. Rather, another Unicorn must have arrived on the scene.

A powerful one.

I spotted the source of the advanced Sapphire magic as Sebastian galloped into view. His unmistakable bi-colored eyes cut through the darkness as his presence dispelled the Corruption weighing in all around us.

I drew in a long breath of air as the pressure lifted.

"Sebastian," I said, knowing that I should have called him Lead General. But I was far too relieved that he'd saved me from an unforgivable sin.

Killing a professor surely was enough to warrant my own death, at the very least. Perhaps a few years of torture, first, knowing Master Nox.

Not to mention Professor Soleil was pretty much the only family I had left. We weren't related, but he treated me like a son, and that meant the world to me.

Tell Guille to stand down, Sebastian ordered.

I hadn't even realized that Guille was about to go

supernova behind me. Sun magic sizzled all around him as his chest heaved. He drew in gulps of air as his fists clenched.

This sort of fight was far too advanced for him, and he was losing control.

Something that I knew would happen, but I'd been naive enough to think I could keep him stabilized.

Running to Guille, I knew I needed to place my hands on him and channel some of the heat into the ground. The Sun House Training Grounds could handle even the worst of a Sun magic burst, but with the Corruption Storm I doubted the area was functioning normally.

When I reached him, I barely grazed his shoulders before pain and heat snapped through my body, forcing me to jolt away. "Fuck!" I cried out as Guille curled in on himself.

He wasn't going to survive like this.

Sebastian cursed behind me, then a wave of cooling water fell from the sky as the ground rumbled and cracked, allowing the worst of the Corruption to bleed through.

Hybrids rarely could handle the mixture of magic, but Sebastian made it look easy. Professor

Soleil writhed on the ground as blue strands of power secured his spirit to his body. The cooling wave washed over him and forced him to fall into a deep, healing sleep.

That was the Sapphire side of Sebastian, as was the cool rain that pattered against my cheeks.

The ground opening up and sucking in the Corruption Storm was his Emerald side. Even the full Emerald House Unicorns that I knew couldn't pull off a feat like this.

But, as Master Nox's brother, Sebastian had a lot to live up to. I didn't envy his life.

He took a few steps toward Guille, then lowered his head until his horn was only a few inches away.

It lit up with a soft blue, forcing Guille's magic to cool.

Guille snapped out of it as the golden gleam finally bled from his eyes. "Oh, fuck. Lead General, I'm so sorry…"

Don't apologize, Sebastian snapped in our minds.

Even if Guille didn't have the skill to communicate telepathically, a skilled Unicorn like Sebastian could force it into anyone's mind by sheer force of will.

He jerked his head, sending his long mane

flinging over his flank. *Just help me get the Professor to the Hold.* He took a step toward me, his Emerald eye facing me as the ground rumbled in warning. *And get me a damn crystal.*

BONNY

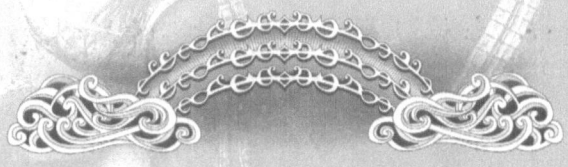

"DID YOU HEAR SOMETHING?" I asked as I pushed away my clean plate.

Raze had been far too good to me, feeding me steak, French Onion soup, pizza, and even M&M's on my request. I shouldn't have been surprised he knew exactly what all those things were, given that he'd come to Earth to find me in the first place.

Normally I'd want Skittles… but I was afraid that the Awakening Ceremony had ruined my favorite candy. So I opted for chocolate candies as a safe bet for now.

"Hmm?" Raze asked as he stared at me.

My cheeks heated under his scrutiny. Needing to have something to do with my hands, I grabbed one of the glasses of bubbly liquid and sipped it.

The ground had definitely been rumbling a moment ago, but I was still trying to process the fact that Raze had told me he was a virgin.

Of course, there wasn't anything wrong with that. I just found it extremely difficult to believe.

But ever since he'd made that admission he'd been at ease, as if telling me the truth had been the right thing to do, and he'd proceeded to distract me with any food I could possibly desire.

Now that I was sated—in every form of the word —I was feeling brave enough to dig for answers.

Deciding that the ground rumbling had been my imagination, or just evidence of my frayed nerves, I blurted out the first question that came to mind.

"Are you gay?" I asked, then clapped a hand over my mouth.

He blinked at me a few times. "What?"

Great. Now I sound like an idiot and *a homophobe.* "I-I mean, you said you were a virgin. I don't see how that's possible." I made a waving motion in his general direction. "Look at you."

He was wearing a pair of loose pants that didn't do a good job of hiding his sizable—and hard— package. While he was wearing a shirt, it was a button-down and the top three buttons had come undone, hinting at his incredible abs.

It took serious effort not to peel the fabric off of him to exactly where all those hard lines went.

Or trace them with my tongue.

I cleared my throat as the errant thought ran through my mind.

I'd decided that magic was definitely responsible for my runaway libido, but Raze also happened to be the most gorgeous male specimen I'd ever seen in my life, or even in my dreams, for that matter.

His ruby-red eyes glowed with a soft light that made him look exotic and alluring. His rainbow hair suited him, brushed over his eyes in a messy way, making me want to run my fingers through it.

High cheekbones and a strong jaw were positively kissable—and *bitable.*

He seemed to enjoy the attention because he offered me a dazzling grin. "I take it you find me attractive?"

That's an understatement.

"Girls would be throwing themselves at you," I replied without directly answering his question.

I felt that was obvious. He was fuckably gorgeous.

He's a walking sex Skittle.

I chuckled at the thought, then covered it up with a cough.

If he noticed my peculiar behavior, he ignored it. "I wouldn't know," he admitted as he waved his hand over the empty plate. Magic glittered with fiery embers until perfectly plump strawberries appeared.

Then glazed over in chocolate.

With multicolor glitter dust.

My mouth watered looking at the treat even though I was impossibly full.

He's trying to distract me with sugar.

And it was working.

"What do you mean by that?" I asked, dragging my gaze away from the conjured confection back to his magnetizing eyes.

He shrugged. "No female Unicorn Shifters, remember?"

Right.

Then I scrunched my nose. "Then how do you guys... procreate?" That seemed to roll my question back to my original tactless query. Maybe Unicorns were asexual creatures, or maybe they didn't need females somehow to produce offspring.

He laughed. The low, delicious sound went straight between my legs. "That's complicated, but we need females of another species to procreate. My mother was an angel, although that's not typical. Usually, the Broodmares are a different type of shifter or even human. It doesn't particularly matter since the Stallion's Unicorn genetics will take over any conceived males."

I stared at him and tried to unpack all of that.

He was part angel, which, given the idea that Unicorns were pure creatures, wasn't too surprising.

Except I hadn't even known angels were able to procreate.

And then there was the fact that he'd just used words like "Broodmare" and "Stallion."

Nope. Does not compute.

He winced. "Sorry. I'm not used to having to explain all this from scratch. Most Unicorn Shifters come to the Academy with a basic understanding of their origins." He picked up one of the strawberries by the stem, then offered it to me. "How about I address your first question. I don't know how to answer because I don't have a sexual identity that I'm aware of." His tongue flashed out over his lower lip as his gaze dipped, longing entering his gaze. "In fact, I've never felt sexual desire until... you." His gaze lifted to mine again, but I'd forgotten how to breathe.

SEBASTIAN

IT WAS ALMOST dawn by the time we reached the Hold, or what was more kindly referred to as the guest wing.

Unicorns hadn't accepted guests in thousands of years, minus a few rare exceptions.

We used the guest wing for detention, the sick, and to otherwise contain anyone we needed to keep under control.

Status update, my brother's voice ordered in my mind.

Based on the weakness of the words, he was well on the other side of campus, maybe even beyond the barrier. Yet, as the Master of the Academy, he had access to more Purity magic than most of us, allowing him to communicate over long distances as he saw fit without the aid of an artifact or hologram panel.

Professor Soleil has been Corrupted and I'm about to take him into the Hold, I said; then unwisely added, *I'll be sure to let the Elders know on my next report that you were nowhere to be found.*

It wasn't wise to provoke my brother, but I could have used his help. It'd taken every ounce of my strength to compel my Sapphire Purity magic to bind Professor Soleil's spirit to his body when he should have died.

Guille had actually been the reason for my success. His wild unleash of raw power gave me something to work with.

But Samuel had nearly cost the Professor his life. He didn't know Corruption's dark secret.

It changed everything it touched, if not fully burned out. Raze would more than likely survive it, given he was a thousand years old and was from the most powerful lineage of our kind.

Professor Soleil, though, had clearly been overwhelmed by the force enough to be changed.

I wasn't sure if he could even be saved, but perhaps he could be studied.

I didn't tell Samuel that's why I'd saved him instead of letting him die.

Go right on ahead, my brother sneered. *I'm bringing what's left of our Guardians back alive from their failed trek to locate Khimaira.*

Shifting into my human form, I frowned and hauled Professor Soleil over my shoulder.

Of course the Elders cared more about a stupid rare monster than they did about a breach. I wasn't going to argue with Nox. He was so far up the Elders' asses that he probably knew what they'd eaten for dinner.

Nox wanted to become an Elder one day. I was fairly certain about that. Which meant what the Elders cared about, he cared about.

I knew the Elders didn't give two shits about the Guardians we could have lost. We'd already lost so many. What were a few more to ancient beings like the Elders?

Khimaira, though, was a one-of-a-kind.

Still, I planned on having a word with the Elders myself. If the Academy fell to Corruption, there won't be anybody to keep their precious monsters in check.

"Do you want any help?" Samuel asked me. He

adjusted the leather bag over his shoulder to get it out of the way. He made a move to help me with the Professor and offered me a hand.

"No," I sharply barked at him. Both he and Guille kept their distance from me, but I didn't have the patience right now to spare their feelings.

They were mere foals compared to me, but I needed them to grow up.

Fast.

"I'm going to move Professor Soleil into a reinforced room," I informed them. "And you're going to find Eli and help him charge those crystals." Eli had only asked for one, but I'd made sure that Samuel had brought all he could carry.

I very much doubted that this latest blight of Corruption was done with us yet.

And I had a bad feeling that this was just the beginning of our problems.

Venturing into the building, I dragged Professor Soleil using brute strength. I didn't need to use my magic to carry him. At my age, I was capable of lifting ten times my weight without breaking a sweat.

Although I did keep a steady stream of my Sapphire magic wrapped around the Professor. It glowed with brilliant blue strands to keep him sedated.

Black blood oozed from his wound and was probably infecting me right now, but I'd already committed. Eli would have been a better Unicorn to charge the crystals, but now it was up to Samuel. Once Samuel charged his crystals, I could burn any Corruption out of my system.

Except, the air felt heavy and wrong the moment I reached the occupied rooms.

"Open that one," I instructed to Guille.

He complied and yanked open the iron-rein-forced door. Iron magnified our magic and would keep my Sapphire hold on Professor Soleil intact until I could come back for him.

Settling him on the bed inside, I brushed my fingers over the scar on my forehead to release my magic.

The room released a *ping* in response, securing everything inside the room in suspended animation.

It wouldn't last forever, perhaps a few days, but it would do for now.

That done, I went to Raze's room first.

I forgot that I hadn't summoned myself any clothes, so when I yanked open the door I stood there like an idiot.

But I couldn't move.

Because Raze was feeding Bonny chocolate-covered strawberries.

And the room smelled like sex. I knew that scent even though I was a virgin. I'd been to the human realm enough times to recognize the mixture of sweat and satisfaction.

Peaches and cream.

My mouth watered at Bonny's unmistakable scent.

Raze's spicy Ruby magic hinted at cherries and caramel that complimented Bonny's aroma.

She glanced at me with her mouth open and her teeth halfway sunk into one of the strawberries.

Her gaze dipped to my cock that instantly went rigid, the mingling scents hitting me hard.

"What the ever-loving fuck is going on here?" I roared.

Samuel peered around me. "I have no idea, but I want to be a part of it."

Turning to glower at him, I found Guille retreating to the adjacent room. "Uh, guys?" he said as he opened the door. "You're going to want to see this."

To be continued in Unicorn Shifter Academy:
Book 2!
Turn the page for a Book 2 Preview!

BOOK 2 PREVIEW: ELI

KEEP YOUR SHIT TOGETHER...

"Eli? Can you hear me?"

A faraway voice called my name. I couldn't register who'd said it, only that I wanted to tell them to get away from me.

To run.

To hide.

Before something terrible happened.

A guttural sound escaped my throat in an attempt to warn the male who had entered my room. I could just make out the golden yellow of a Sun Unicorn's eyes.

It would have been better to encounter Raze's ruby gaze, but Samuel would have to suffice.

The crystals... I thought as numbness threatened to take over my weakened mind.

Pain sliced up my arms and down my spine as the Corruption took hold.

There was no coming back from this. I knew that the change was permanent.

I was touched by darkness.

I could never return to my life as a Guardian.

"Hold on," Samuel said as he held up an empty crystal.

The damn thing wasn't even charged, and he thought that was going to be able to save me?

He should be worrying about himself.

The best I could do to warn him was another animalistic growl, and then my bones snapped.

It wasn't to change into my Unicorn form. That sort of shift wasn't painful and required magic over physical transformation.

But this change was different. It *hurt*, and it filled me with rage.

The faint scent of peaches and cream infiltrated the metallic mist of the room, but it wasn't enough to distract me from my new goal.

My vision had darkened, but now it cleared as I focused my entire being on the Sun Unicorn. He glowed with life and vibrance, something that gravely offended me right now.

End him, a voice told me with a seductive quality.

Until Bonny, I'd never been lured like this. And now, this voice put me under its spell in much the same way.

A hunger filled me. One that demanded I tear the flesh from bone and devour anything that held life and magic.

A Sun Unicorn held both in abundance.

My knees bent the wrong way, giving me a springboard effect as my tails elongated into claws. Fangs pressed against my lips and a singular horn protruded from my head.

It wasn't my golden horn that housed all my magic and glory. The Corruption had taken that from me. Instead, a twisted onyx spiral jutted from my skull with a deadly sharp end.

"Eli!" Samuel futility shouted.

Others entered the room, but I didn't take note of them. I'd already set my sights on my target.

They would die next.

Yes. Devour them, Eli. Feed me.

Feed us.

And then you will be free.

The voice held a promise that I couldn't ignore.

Even if I hadn't been enraptured, the hunger raking through my core propelled me to act in the most violent way possible.

Snarling, I launched for Samuel while he desperately tried to power the crystal in his hand. His horn had appeared from his forehead in an impressively controlled shift, but it wouldn't save him. He touched the crystal with his horn, beginning the charging process that he was far too young to pull off.

Not to mention he should be using his horn to defend himself, not futilely try to save me when I was already lost.

My horn impacted something hard and powerful —definitely not the delicious flesh of the Sun Unicorn.

As a shockwave blasted through the room, I twisted from the force and lashed to the side.

Dazed, I finally turned to see who had intervened.

A female with rainbow hair lashing wildly around her face clenched her fists and stood her ground. An impressively large horn glowed from her forehead with incredible power that only a Unicorn well past five hundred years of age should inherit.

She stopped my blow with her horn... impressive.

"Eli," she said, the word stern but also laced with a desperation that forced me to hesitate.

She held out a hand. "Eli, I don't fully understand what's happening right now, but I need you to focus on me. I need you to hold my hand. Can you do that for me?"

Everyone in the room stared at us.

Raze with powerful ruby eyes that blurred with power. He would chop off my head if I so much as flinched. By the looks of the aura glittering all around him, he had fully recovered from his ordeal.

But hadn't he been Corrupted, too?

And why was he allowing this female to talk to me? Did he have so much faith in someone he'd only just met?

I pondered that as I took in my other adversaries.

Guille, Samuel's friend, fumbled with more crystals by the doorway.

Two of the foreign visitors looked out of place as they took a brave stand behind the female. A mermaid shifter and a young warlock wouldn't be much of a challenge against someone like me.

"I... can't." The words croaked out of me with

regret as I bent my legs the wrong way again, my body leaning into a striking pose.

I was glad I couldn't see myself. The female's influence seemed to clear my mind of the Corruption, but she couldn't eradicate it entirely. The change had already reached someplace deep inside.

It shouldn't have been able to reach my soul. My soul had been removed from my body to both serve my realm and to protect myself from losing my powers. With it, I should have been protected by soul-corrupting forces such as creatures of Calamity like this.

The infecting darkness had many names.

Touched.

Malice.

Calamity's Essence.

Shadow, although perhaps a more potent form of it.

There were Dark Mages who could control Shadow, but even they hadn't been able to control this. Not since Ayla, and she wasn't going to help us.

We were on our own.

My vision wavered as the Corruption threatened to take over my mind again, and the hunger returned.

I closed my eyes. "You need... *to run.*"

NOTE FROM THE AUTHOR

Thank you for reading the first installment of Unicorn Shifter Academy!

This book was exactly what I needed right now. Life has been hectic and my muse has been struggling to find joy among all of the heavy writing deadlines and daily tasks.

Somewhere among the spreadsheets and marketing emails a Unicorn found me. It all started with a unicorn bunny in Fortune Academy with a backstory bigger than I ever could have imagined.

Uni didn't make an appearance in this book, but he was what originally inspired Unicorn Shifter Academy and ultimately played such a key role in the resolution of Calamity.

Fortune Academy is one of those series that blew up in size and is the culmination of multiple converging storylines. In order to understand how the massive series ends, I needed to write the first books of Moon Guardian and Unicorn Shifter Academy to fully grasp it.

Now that Unicorn Shifter Academy has been introduced, I'm able to finish Fortune Academy fully knowing where this world has gone. I have a very different writing style than many authors, so I appreciate my readers who dive into the unicorn rabbit hole with me!

To fully appreciate this series, I recommend going back and reading all of the books in this world before you head onto Unicorn Shifter Academy: Book Two and beyond. If you look up the books on Amazon, you'll be able to scroll down and find the recommended reading order and make sure you're all caught up!

Series	Series 1	Series 2	Series 3	Series 4	Series 5	Series 6
	Seven Sins	The Vampire Curse	Fortune Academy	Dark Arts Academy	Moon Guardian: Crescent Five	Unicorn Shifter Academy

Thank you and see you next time in Unicorn Shifter Academy: Book Two!

J.R. Thorn

Reverse Harem Paranormal Romance - Never Choose.

J.R. Thorn is a Reverse Harem Paranormal Romance Author who loves coffee, stormy weather, and heated discussions with her inner muse. She can often be found scribing her steamy stories in her writing cave far away from the prying eyes of her toddler, husband, two vocal cats, and one distracting Pomsky pup.

www.AuthorJRThorn.com

RECOMMENDED READING ORDER

All Books are Standalone Series listed by their sequential order of events

Standalone Stories

Taste Me

Their Blood Queen

Dragonrider Academy

Elemental Fae Universe Reading List

Elemental Fae Academy: Books 1-3

Midnight Fae Academy

Fortune Fae Academy

Fortune Fae M/M Steamy Episodes

Candela

Winter Fae Queen

Hell Fae

Blood Stone Series Universe Reading List

Recommended Reading Order is Below

Seven Sins (Books 1-3)

Book 1: Succubus Sins

Book 2: Siren Sins

Book 3: Vampire Sins

The Vampire Curse: Royal Covens (Books 1-3)

Book 1: Her Vampire Mentors

Book 2: Her Vampire Mentors

Book 3: Her Vampire Mentors

Fortune Academy (Part I)

Year One

Year Two

Year Three

Fortune Academy Underworld (Part II)

Book 3.5: Burn in Hell

Book Four

Book 4.5: Burn in Rage

Book Five

Book Six

Book 6.5: Burn in Brilliance

Fortune Academy Underworld (Part III)

Book Seven

Book Eight

Book 8.5: Burn in Ruin

Book 8.666: Burn in Darkness

Book Nine

Book Ten

Crescent Five

(Rejected Mate Wolf Shifter RH)

Book One: Moon Guardian

Book Two: Moon Cursed

Book Three: Moon Queen

Book Four: Moon Kissed

Dark Arts Academy (Vella)

Ongoing serial

Book One (KU)

Book Two (KU)

Unicorn Shifter Academy

- *Book One*

- *Book Two*

- *Book Three*

Non-RH Books (J.R. Thorn writing as Jennifer Thorn)

Noir Reformatory Universe Reading List

Noir Reformatory: The Beginning (Standalone)

Noir Reformatory: First Offense

Noir Reformatory: Second Offense

Noir Reformatory Turns RH from this point with the addition of a third mate

Noir Reformatory: Third Offense

Sins of the Fae King Universe Reading List

(Book 1) Captured by the Fae King

(Book 2) Betrayed by the Fae King

Learn More at www.AuthorJRThorn.com

Fortune Academy: Year One Sneak Peek

Read Lilith's story featuring her mates, including Hendrik, that you encountered in Dark Arts Academy. The events in Fortune Academy take place before Dark Arts Academy, so make sure you're all caught up! Here's chapter one to get you started...

CHAPTER ONE

It all started with a severed hand and a hot bounty hunter. For the record, I would never chop off the hand of a hot guy... unless he was being a total douchebag—which he was. Plus, it grew back, so it doesn't even really count... not that I was aware bounty hunters could regrow appendages, but hey, no harm no foul.

Right, I tend to blather on without context so let me start from the beginning, right around the time when my memories restarted in the middle of the street with no idea who I was. Boy, was I in for a surprise when I figured that one out.

The first thing I remember from that point on was my clothes sticking to my skin and my hair plastered to my cheeks from the freezing rain. Everything was sore as if I'd been run over by a bulldozer. I wandered, drawn by a pull that promised refuge until I found myself in a dark alley facing the back entrance of a bar. Raindrops hit my face like irritating little insects, but I couldn't seem to find the strength to leave this particular doorstep. Something bad had happened to me and I must have run until I couldn't run anymore. My legs trembled underneath me like jello and my heart wouldn't stop thundering in my ears. All I could do was gulp in breaths of air and wait for someone to open that dull, red door lined with scratches.

The moonlight was too bright, but I peered up at the sky and pleaded for mercy anyway. I didn't know what I needed mercy for, or why I was paralyzed in the freezing rain at this grimy doorstep, but I just knew that this was my last hope. I had to stay here until that door opened.

The streetlights blasted on and made me flinch, but I stared at the door until it opened and a woman in her late forties peered down at me with a disgusted scowl. She stared at me for a long time before she stepped aside. "Come on," she said, then turned around and left the entranceway free.

That's how I became Cindy's newest waitress. Waiting like a drowned rat at the back of her bar to what was supposed to be her secret entrance reserved for smoke breaks. Well, that's how all supernaturals found Cindy. Now when I walked outside I could spot the little ugly engraving in the corner of the doorway that drew people like me to the place. A little tiny skull etched there with a dumb grin on its face like it knew how many headaches it would bring Cindy. This was her punishment... to help people like me who had no memory of who they were or what they'd done. Ever since the Second Echo of Calamity apparently the world had gone to all sorts of shit and supernaturals had to start over with clean slates, memories included. What Cindy had done to deserve her fostering of looney supernaturals, I had no idea and she wasn't about to admit it to me.

The thing was, Cindy attracted just that, supernaturals. Sure, something was off about me, but even I felt like I didn't quite fit in with the supernatural crowd of misfits. I had a feeling that my memory loss didn't have much to do with the whacky weirdness that was going on with the world. It was something more personal... but Cindy didn't have to know that.

I liked Cindy. She never asked questions or gave me a hard time when I didn't seem to know basic things. It felt like I had to learn how to live life all over again. Something fundamental had changed in me and I couldn't put my finger on what. Without having any memory of my past, I wasn't even going to try and figure it out. Let it come naturally, that's what Cindy always said.

We had this weird kind of understanding that made our relationship work. I'd shown up on her doorstep in the middle of the night covered in blood and soaked with rain and she'd taken me in just like she'd done with so many before me.

That's what the mother of monsters always did.

"Guy at table three has been ogling you for an hour," Jess told me as she balanced a tray on her hip.

Jess was the closest thing I had to a friend in the same way that Cindy was the closest thing I had to a mother. Jess had arrived only a few weeks before I did, but she was already well on her way to recovery. Cindy had set up a few interviews for Jess at various escort gigs. Normally I'd disapprove, but Jess seemed to love the attention, so I hoped she would be happy when it was time for her to go.

"Don't be a bimbo," I said, making a point to ignore the guy she'd pointed out. "No way he's looking at me when you're standing right here." I gave her short skirt and halter top a raised brow. She already had voluptuous boobs and a rounded ass big enough to make a guy stop in his tracks, and that outfit made everything pop in just the right way. "I'm not a succubus like you."

She grinned, showing off her pearly white teeth. "I'm serious, Lily, he's checking you out!"

Dread washed over me. I had the good looks, sure. Long, blonde hair, legs that could kill in some heels and plump lips that would be perfect for pouting... if I ever pouted, which I didn't. I desperately hoped that I wasn't a succubus.

I still didn't know what I was yet, which was frustrating, but since being a succubus was still on the table I scanned the bar just for good measure. Every guy in the place was drooling over Jess and making a fool of themselves... every guy except for the one at table three.

Our gazes matched long enough for a jolt of familiar awareness to slam through me.

Okay, that was weird.

I tried to pretend I was fascinated with my phone. "I'm off duty, Jess," I reminded her as I scrolled through a mindless social media thread. "Go give the guy a new beer. The one you gave him an hour ago looks flat and he's probably just thirsty."

"Yeah," she snickered and waggled her eyebrows, "thirsty for some of your lo-ove," she said, making sure to sing-song the last word.

Ignoring her, I continued to scroll through my phone. It wasn't hard to pretend my fascination when the damn thing was so addictive. Cindy allowed me to use it as long as it was only for "research," as she called it. I never called anyone or posted anything online. I loved to read about humans and see what kinds of things they shared with each other. Most of it involved vague statements I didn't understand, pictures of kittens— which I always approved of—and snaps of perfectly arranged meals. Then there was the occasional political post about the emergence of supernaturals. Everyone had an opinion, especially when it came to Fortune Academy. *A Place Where Supernaturals Belong.* That was their slogan.

When I'd asked Cindy about it, she'd sneered and told me that if I was smart, I'd steer clear of anything related to that place.

Not that I was going to tell Cindy my opinion, but she had to be wrong. An entire organization dedicated to helping lost supernaturals? While I appreciated all that Cindy did for me, she didn't have answers. Fortune Academy would give me a fighting chance at figuring out what the hell I was.

One slight problem… the academy had stringent perquisites to join, one of which is demonstrating a supernatural ability—which I hadn't been able to do yet. I only knew I was supernatural because I'd lost my memories and Cindy's door rune had called me to her.

I'd figure out what I was… but it wasn't going to be easy.

Jess elbowed me in the ribs. "Hey, are you listening to me?"

I rolled my eyes. "You're still here? I said I was busy."

She leaned in and lowered her voice, not taking her eyes off the stranger. "I really think you should go talk to him, Lils. I can tell when a guy has the hots, and while he definitely has the hots for you, something is off about him that I can't really figure out. I don't like it."

I chuckled. "I'll tell you what's off about him. There's a gorgeous succubus in the room and he's staring at me. Clearly the guy's missing some marbles." And of course she didn't like it. Jess needed to get all of the male attention—which was fine with me.

"Hey, sweet cheeks!" A guy from across the bar yelled at Jess. "You bringing me those beers, or what?"

Jess waved at him and giggled, which just pissed me off. "You should go kick that guy in the balls."

Jess huffed and readjusted her tray. "That's not how I get the good tips. Now go talk to the hottie at table three or I will." She pursed her lips and gave me a you-better-go-talk-to-him-or-else look and then marched over to deliver the impatient human his beers.

I turned my attention back to the topic of our discussion. The stranger hunched into himself, hiding his face in the shadow of his cowl. I frowned.

That either meant he was shy, or he was hiding something.

Someone who could resist a succubus' charms wasn't the shy type, so I stuffed my phone in the back of my jeans pocket and marched over to his table. I crossed my arms until he grunted at me.

"Oh, so you can talk?" I snapped. Irritation put me on edge. I was standing right in front of him and he wouldn't look up at me. "What, you can stare at me all night when I'm halfway across the room but when I come to your table you've got nothing to say?"

He twisted the untouched beer that Jess had delivered to him an hour ago, leaving a ring of condensation on the table. "So, you don't remember me." His voice came out husky and low... and apparently he knew who I was.

My entire body froze and a cold sweat broke out on my face. I'd harbored the secret hope that someone might recognize me in a popular bar, but I'd also feared the day someone who knew me might show up. I'd arrived at a monster's orphanage... and I'd been soaked in more than icy rain that night I'd shown up at Cindy's doorstep.

Yes I'd been covered in blood—but it was blood that wasn't my own. By the time I got my clothes off that night and slipped into a borrowed set of pajamas, I discovered I didn't have a single scratch on me.

I somehow managed to swallow the bitter fear that crawled up my throat. Letting out a nervous laugh, I flipped my hair over my shoulder. Guys always reacted better when they thought I was a dumb blonde. "Sorry. Maybe if you weren't hiding behind your cowl I could actually see your face, you know? Hard to jostle the memory with just a broody voice."

He hesitated and then shifted so that his cowl moved just enough for me to see the hard ridge of his chin. "I don't brood," he growled.

It was almost cute how he immediately retorted the insult. I was about to make it worse, but then he pulled back his hood all the way and hot damn, the guy was smoking.

And, well, his eyes glowed with a metallic orange magic that marked him as a supernatural bounty hunter... but yeah, details.

I shouldn't have been surprised that a bounty hunter would show up at Cindy's bar, but he still managed to take me off guard. While my mind was mush, my body reacted to the deadly flash of silver that was his blade. The world around me stilled with a magical lock. I didn't know if it was something I'd done or if it had been the bar's defenses. Taking advantage of the moment, I twisted to put as much distance as possible between me and the hunter.

Except... he tracked my movements with ease, his eyes locked onto mine as I moved. When I flinched, he flicked the blade and its merciless silver etched across my vision. I knew it would be sharp enough to cut my head clean off my body, but I realized a half-second too late that he hadn't been aiming for me.

Jess cried out and clutched at the embedded hilt, crumpling to the floor as time unlocked from its slowed momentum.

"Jess!" I screamed and lurched to her aid, but the hunter had me by the arm with a vice grip.

"You're welcome," he growled and tugged me into his chest. "She was about to kill you."

Flattened against his hard abs, I curled my fingers into the thick layers of his coat and peered up at him, taking in the full brutal force of his hard edges and glowing eyes. Everything about him screamed danger, but the way he held me was protective... almost gentle.

A clatter of metal hit the floor and broke a silence that I realize didn't make any sense in a crowded bar. No one seemed to notice that Jess had been stabbed, or that a hunter with glowing eyes was holding me.

That was because time was frozen... but not Jess.

Jess... who now had a dagger plunged in her chest.

Even a succubus should have died from a mortal wound like that, but she snarled as if irritated by the blade and launched for me. The hunter reacted before I did and held out his hand to defend me, which would have been sweet, except the weapon struck clean through flesh and bone, severing his hand and sending it flopping to the floor like a lump of meat.

"Oh dear..." I murmured.

He cursed and wrapped the stumped remains of his hand in his cloak. When Jess cried out and collapsed to her knees, I realized that he hadn't cursed under his breath, but rather cast a spell.

So, my bounty hunter had some magical mojo.

"You bastard!" Jess screamed. "She's mine!"

My brain couldn't process Jess screaming at the hunter, so my gaze wandered throughout the bar that was like a snapshot in time.

A group three tables down held up their beers in celebration and one sloshed his contents into the air, the foam and droplets making a perfect arc over his friend's head.

Cars outside that should have been speeding down the dark alleyway were now stopped. The one closest to the window featured a woman with her hair fanned out behind her as if she was trapped in a photoshoot.

Then I spotted Cindy watching from the back

with the door cracked open. Even she was trapped in the moment. Whatever had frozen time, only the hunter, Jess, and I were able to move. It bothered me more that Cindy was just back there... watching... as if waiting for something to happen. If she knew who the hunter was, why wouldn't she have stopped me from talking to him?

The hunter shook me with his remaining hand. He should have been buckled over in pain, but I didn't know much about bounty hunters. Maybe he could shut his pain off. "You need to stop daydreaming," he snapped. "Look." He pointed and my gaze obeyed even though my brain didn't want to process what was going on.

A knife rested on the ground just inches from Jess's hand, but not the one the hunter had stabbed her with. That one was still lodged in her chest and blood pooled around the wound and seeped into her clothing.

"Jess?" I asked, my voice cracking when I finally realized that she'd been coming at us with a knife. Not just any knife, but a blade etched with runes that glowed red.

I considered Jess my friend, even though I'd only been here a few weeks and was still trying to remember who I was. Cindy told me that I shouldn't rush it. Just take as much time as I needed. Jess had always been supportive in her own way, but this wasn't the Jess who talked to me about guys or stole a shot with me from behind the bar. She gripped the hilt of the dagger still embedded in her chest and glared at me. I'd never seen anyone look at me with such hatred, much less someone I thought was my friend.

"You're a monster," she said, almost like it was something she'd kept in for far too long. "You're supposed to work for us. No one else can have you!" She lurched for the dagger she'd dropped, but cried out in pain and slapped her hand on the floor.

If it hadn't been for the hunter who still held me with one strong arm, I would have gone ice cold. I hadn't been in many situations where I was this stressed, but sometimes when a customer got rowdy or Cindy raised her voice my fingertips would go so cold that they'd feel numb until I grabbed onto someone. Now the urge to touch devoured me worse than I'd ever felt it and I crawled my hands up the hunter's clothes until I reached a patch of skin exposed at his neck. He flinched the moment my icy fingers met his, but he didn't stop me. Instead he stroked my hair out of my eyes and gave me a sobering look.

"It's Lily, right?"

Hearing my name jolted me into awareness and I looked into his eyes that still glowed with that fascinating metallic golden gleam. "Uh, yeah." How did he know my name?

He surveyed the bar and frowned. "I can't hold the time lock once we step outside of this bar. We're lucky that the monster mother was on the other side of the door when I initiated it." He glanced down at the dagger still in Jess's chest. I noticed one gem on the end of the hilt glowing green, but that light was starting to fade. "We don't have much longer. Do you think you can move?"

The shock of what he was proposing made all the heat I'd gathered into my fingertips surge straight through my whole body. He jerked away from me and cursed.

"You can't mean that I'd go somewhere with you?" I asked.

"Yes," he growled, transforming from the kind and patient stranger I'd been clinging to back into the hunter that had come to... what had he come here to do? "If you stay here you'll be killed... or worse. You have to come with me."

Sense came back to me as I bristled. No one told

me what to do. "I can take care of myself, thank you very much."

"You better listen to him," Jess drawled, grinning manically as her eyelids drooped and blood tinted her teeth pink. It was the most terrifying sight I'd ever seen, especially since one side of her face was starting to droop and one of her eyes was turning black. "I'm not really a succubus, you know. I'm something else... something even better. I wasn't ready to show you, but looks like I don't have a choice. You lost your memory because you weren't ready to learn what you are, but I've embraced it."

"You shut your mouth," the hunter snapped and produced a second blade. "Lily is nothing like you."

She gurgled on another laugh. "Oh, protective, are you? Didn't come to kill her... but to collect her for your little academy? How quaint."

I dug my fingernails into my palm. The air around us started to tremble as if the whole world was about to fall apart. I couldn't leave Jess here, dying, even if she was frightening me. I didn't care what she was, I needed to give her a chance to explain. Maybe if she thought I wouldn't go with him she'd stop trying to attack me.

She gave me a look of pity. Which was incredulous. Jess, the one with the knife in her chest and her face falling apart, gave *me* a look of pity. "Such a sweet thing. You still want to help me, don't you?" She sighed. "Tricky blood you have. Two-thirds of you is perfect for Monster Academy, but there's that nasty little extra third that shows its ugly head. I see it right now in your eyes. No proper monster would look at me like that." Her face twisted with rage. "Mother will burn it out of you. Then you can join us and Monster Academy will finally have its star pupil." She chuckled. "Or failed experiment. Either way, I will be getting some major extra credit for this."

"Monster Academy?" I shrieked. "Jess, what the hell are you talking about?"

She opened her mouth to answer me, but a loud crack reverberated through the room and time unlocked from its latch.

"Time to go," the hunter said and took me by the arm again.

Everything happened all at once. The serene silence dropped into a clatter of noise typical of a busy bar. Startled, I ducked as if the bombardment of sounds was an object hurled at my head, and good thing, too. Cindy burst through the door and launched fire—fucking fire!—from her hand.

I'd never seen anything like it. The flames were

so hot that they melted straight through a pair of guests and sent their corpses disintegrating to the floorboards. The bar exploded and the scent of fear hit me like a wall.

"Come on!" the hunter shouted and tugged at me, but I was rooted to the spot. He gave me a look of surprise.

That's right. I was supernatural. No fucking idea what I was, but he wasn't going to move me unless I agreed to it.

Which, going with him was starting to feel like a good idea. Jess was talking about hooking me up with Monster Academy—no idea what that was but it didn't sound good—and Cindy was throwing fire around and killing people.

I had a decision to make and not much time to make it. One quick glance at Jess gave me mixed feelings. She clearly wasn't a succubus. Jess's beauty melted off of her as if the dagger in her chest drained her of her outer skin. I wasn't sure if it had been a spell or some elaborate magical sleeve, but whatever this creature was before me now with black eyes and wrinkled skin was the real Jess.

Strangely, I wanted to get to know her. Those black eyes still had Jess inside of them. There was more darkness and pain, but still the friend that I'd come to care for.

Yet, when she went for the cool blade again on the floor, I knew that she would rather kill me than let the hunter have me. Perhaps I was naive, just like she always told me I was.

Closing my eyes with resignation, I let the hunter haul me out of the bar and into the cold night.

Of course, it was fucking raining, and the blood on me wasn't my own.

www.ingramcontent.com/pod-product-compliance
Lightning Source LLC
Chambersburg PA
CBHW031948240626
47153CB00003B/900